Not My
BACHELOR

by
Tricia Heggeness

Olympus Story House

Contents

I dedicate this book to my two beautiful daughters, Greta and Lisa. Without them, I would not have followed my dreams to become a fictional writer. Thank you, sweet darlings, for your love and devotion and for believing in me.

Chapter 1

"So how long will you be gone?"

"Indefinitely," I say quickly.

At the young age of 27, my short adult life is profoundly balanced with a mixture of romance and luck. Unlike many recent college graduates; I had no difficulty finding employment. After spending an internship at a small magazine called *Lifestyle in NYC* during my senior year at NYU. Thankful to the powers from above, they offered me a position as a freelance writer. That was four years ago, and suffice it to say, they haven't fired me yet.

I live with my boyfriend, Brandon Stacker, whom I met during my undergraduate studies at NYU and who is currently training to become an orthopedic surgeon. He is the one asking me the question about an upcoming trip. My relationship with Brandon has become almost non-existent since he began his orthopedic surgery residency one year ago. He lives and breathes medicine, but I had been forewarned about the long tedious days followed by the outrageous on-call schedule of doctors in training. I can recall every moment when we first met.

I was sitting with four of my college roommates at a typical run-down, seedy cramped campus bar located near our freshman dormitory when a group of the nerdiest upper-class boys sauntered by our table. My friends and I noticed them immediately with their too-short cropped hair, their awkward and gangly inability to try to look cool, and the fact they each carried a classroom textbook. Of course, a classic of 18-year-old girls, we started giggling which made the boys stop and exchange looks with us. When my eyes locked with Brandon's, I felt an immediate kinetic connection. I have never felt anything like that before.

Much to my youthful delight, his dreamy blue eyes, framed by dark-rimmed Superman glasses, lit up and his boyish chiseled face turned a pale shade of crimson. His right hand reached up to wipe a non-existent piece of hair away from his eyes. And then he gave me a flirtatious smile, and I knew right then I was burnt toast. It was also obvious to my new friends.

"Rina? Rina? Katarina Spencer, did you hear a word I just said?" yelled Lori.

Startling me out of my dreamy stupor, I looked at Lori and said, "Did you just say something?"

"Yes, I just told you an entire story about my most embarrassing moment, and I will never repeat it again," Lori said, indignantly pouting. "Where did you go? I thought the reason for us coming here was to get better acquainted." She was right. I share a dormitory room with three girls at NYU with whom I have never met before.

"I am sorry, but for some reason, one of those boys has intrigued me, and my senses are not easily aroused." I then regaled them about my past disastrous high-school relationships and the four of us relaxed, and we spent the next hour thinking up ways for me to say 'hi' to him. Which I did, since I have never been bashful before. Ever since that day, we have been girlfriend and boyfriend. We were known as 'Brina', no longer Brandon and Rina. We breathed as one. Until now.

But, luckily, I am a very independent girl and have no problem keeping myself busy. On weekends, most of my free time is spent trying to make our teeny loft apartment, located on the Upper East Side of Manhattan, a home. The eclectic antique furnishings give the loft an appearance of antiquated old, mixed with a modern touch all my own. But my real challenge lies with the pasty-white painted brick walls with a cottage cheese surface. Nothing, no matter what type of product or nail I try, penetrates the wall, so hanging up any pictures or photos has been a chore.

It has become an ongoing joke between Brandon and me, and lately, I don't think it's very funny. I almost feel sorry for the neighbors below us because I have tried countless times to hang something on the wall only to return to our loft a few hours later to find the photo or picture scattered in pieces on the putty gray concrete floor. Can you imagine the noise that carries down to the floor below us?

New York City is no stranger to me. I was born and raised on Long Island and have friends scattered near and far. However, my only sister Susannah lives in Southern California along with my ailing mother, who has recently been diagnosed with untreatable lung cancer. So, today, at the end of March, I am trying to decide which clothes to pack for the visit.

As I look outside and see the freezing rain pelting my apartment windows, add that to the fact the storm will intensify during the night, I can't help but shudder, wrapping my arms around myself trying to keep warm. Fortunately, when I peruse the weather app on my cell phone, I realized there was no doubt in my mind that the temperature will be much warmer in sunny southern California.

Tonight, I get to spend some "us time" with Brandon since he promised to come home early. Usually, he doesn't get home until long after I have fallen soundly asleep. After I packed, repacked, and threw in some extra clothes I probably will never wear, Brandon walks back into our apartment carrying a bottle of champagne. Watching me pack is not high on his list, so after a half hour of boundless decision-making on my part, as I toss clothes into the suitcase, he decided to run an errand.

"Honey, I am home." Brandon walks back into our apartment. I didn't question his whereabouts, but I am extremely pleased with his purchase. After pouring each of us a glass of costly and over-rated Dom Perignon champagne into our mismatched wine glasses, we decide to search the television for something besides the news. It is already 10:00 pm, so our selection is limited.

Channel surfing, I come across this television reality show that some of my friends have raved about, but I personally have never watched, called "Love at First Sight". It's a show in which bachelors and bachelorettes go on pre-arranged dates and, hopefully, fall in love. Now considering my own experience, I do believe in "Love at First Sight," but not when a live audience at the end of the show gets to make that choice. Awkward, don't you think? But for some reason, it has been on the air for eight seasons, and I read that it has a success rate of 60%.

Brandon immediately vetoes the show and grabs the remote to switch to another channel. We cuddle up on our little hand-me-down comfy couch with a crocheted afghan and begin to watch another episode of *Breaking Bad*. It is one of those shows that both he and I can enjoy together, not a girly show at all. After the show, Brandon whispers into my ear, "Aren't you glad we don't have to worry about first dates."

Agreeing with him, I pull him closer, our lips and tongues searching as my pulse races and instantly aligns with his rapidly beating heart. The kiss is not the worshiping collaboration of two tongues, but the staggering hunger of two people desperately trying to get the most out of this passionate reunion.

Recognizing the familiar expansion of his pants, both of us are cognizant of each other's arousal; wild, excited desire builds up to the point that the insistent brush of his thumb over my breast creates an urgency, heightening my hunger inside. Following his lead, my fingertips follow a path that travels his entire body.

Before I can recover from our breathtaking union, the material of our clothes rubbing against each other, Brandon methodically peels each article of clothing from both of us. He lifts me to him to enter inside. His tempo matching mine, we both lie together cocooned in unrivaled throbbing sensations. Our hunger is so acute and unexpected; we both feel weak, limp, and totally conquered as Brandon pulls me tightly into his arms and whispers, "Wow, I should come home early more often."

***

When my ride share drops me off at Susannah's house the next day, I continue to be stunned by its simple beauty. The Mediterranean-style ranch house oozes money and class, beginning with the gray stone circular driveway bordered by colorful red and yellow peonies, continuing on with the immaculate hilly desert-like landscape with oversized boulders scattered around the pathway which further leads to the enormous etched glass and wrought iron front door. Nervous as always, I ring the doorbell.

If you think I am living a dream, my sister lives an unbelievable life. Susannah is married to one of the smartest men I know, besides, of course, Brandon. Well, let me explain. When I first met Brandon, he looked like a nerd, but once I talked to him, I could see that besides his obvious intelligence, he had a funny and charming nature about him that makes you laugh. Now when you meet Susannah's husband Alex, he is the true definition of nerd and brains—serious by nature, with thick black glasses, a long, straight European nose, beady black eyes, and wiry black hair that no matter how much pomade he uses, it won't stay down.

Think of Alfalfa, from the Little Rascals, and then multiply his little hair mishap by ten. And, when I talk to him, I feel so small and inadequate because he knows so much about everything. His presence makes me feel as if I am being transported back in time and find myself sitting in a college freshman lecture hall. But my sister adores him, and I can't help but respect and admire how smart he is. That's why he works for one of the biggest computer software companies in the Los Angeles area and makes more money than Donald Trump.

Hence, the house and my nervousness.

The maid Mary opens the door and beams when she sees me. "I thought you were one of those bloody solicitors," she said in her crisp British accent.

"Susannah, Katarina is finally here!" she yells. I can hear the rapid sound of click clack come nearer and then she appears. She looks adorable in a pair of white leggings and a navy-blue and white striped silk tunic, complemented with matching blue sandals.

"Rina, Mom, and I are so excited you are here. She has been in a tizzy all morning knowing that you were on your way. You know how she feels about airplanes." Kissing me on both of my cheeks, Susannah backs away, twirls in a full circle, and asks, "Do you notice anything different?"

My eyes travel up to her hair to see if maybe she colored, cut, or styled her hair differently. No, that isn't it. I stare at her hands and her feet, but nothing pops into my mind.

"No, sorry. What has changed? You look as beautiful as always." And that is the truth. Susannah has this look about her that reminds most people of a southern belle—from her shoulder-length curly blond hair, down to her milky white skin and startling cornflower-blue eyes. Unlike myself, who has straight brown hair, olive-toned skin, and light green eyes, most people cannot tell we are sisters.

Pouting, she looks at me with these huge sad eyes. "Look again." Mind you, I am extremely tired because I have traveled five hours on a plane, two hours just to get through the extremely long lines at security before the flight, and another hour in the backseat of a too-small car with an over-talkative Uber driver. Do we really have to do this? I just look at her with this blank stare.

Susannah stomps her right foot. "Geez, Rina, can't you tell I have a little bump right here." And she points to her stomach and then turns to show me her belly profile.

At last, I got it. We hug as I say, "Oh my goodness, Susannah, you are pregnant. I am so happy for you. How many months are you because I can barely see that lovely bump?"

"Almost three months, and I can't wait to hold this cuddly child in my arms. I would have told you earlier, but I wanted to tell you in person. Mom is so happy for Alex and me." And then Susannah's eyes well up with tears, which immediately reminds me why I am here.

"How is she? I would have come sooner, but I had to finish up some last-minute work for the magazine. Is she in pain?"

"She is doing well, but why don't you see for yourself."

I follow Susannah as she leads the way. Walking through the octagon foyer, I can't help but glance ahead at the living room with the shiny black lacquered baby grand piano begging for someone to sit down and play, to the two matching floral couches with oversized cushions that sit in front of the floor to ceiling windows overlooking the incredibly white-capped tumultuous Pacific Ocean. Placed strategically on the couches are several decorative pillows that match the sunflower yellow and tangerine orange walls. It is such a lovely room that screams taste, elegance, and beauty.

The kitchen itself is larger than my apartment. The bright white cabinets and the sparkling beige marble floor provide a cheerful ambiance. But what immediately grabs your attention is the enormous U-shaped center island made of black glittery granite.

Ten counter stools surround the island and sitting in one of the stools, with a coffee cup held in her right hand, I almost did not recognize my mother, Rose. Usually, about 130 pounds which is perfect for her 5'5" height, she looks so small and frail. I would guess her weight to be less than 100 lbs. For some reason, I am not expecting this, and my eyes fill with tears.

Pulling up a chair next to her, I take her fragile hand and hold it tight. "Hi, Mom, I missed you so much."

She looks at me and smiles. And, when she smiles, her face illuminates and reminds me of the mother I have known all my life. "Rina, I am so glad you are here. I have been waiting for the three of us to be together for way too long." And then I pull her into my arms, for a hug that I do not want to end.

"That's right, Mom. Just the three of us, of course, minus my twin brothers. The way it has been for a long time when we used to go on our 'just girls' outings. We have a lot to catch up on. What would you like to do first?" I gulp away my tears and then I turn toward my sister who is having a hard time trying to keep her own tears from falling.

My father died 18 years ago, September 11, 2001. He was an NYPD firefighter and was one of the first responders to the Twin Towers. My mother was devastated. He was her life, and it changed dramatically when he died.

She suddenly became a single mother with two daughters (Susannah was in high school, and I was in middle school), and a set of wild and hyperactive twin elementary school-aged boys.

When my father was alive, my mother's main responsibility was to take care of the house, protect us, and love my dad. Those were easy tasks for her. But, once he was gone, she needed to figure out who she was without him. And she did, but with much sacrifice.

She decided to go back to college at the age of 38 and become a nurse. She needed to be needed, she wanted to make a difference, and she had to have a purpose in life. She blossomed as a nurse, receiving several nursing awards. All of us were so proud of her.

So, now as I look at her, I realize how unfair life can be.

"Did I ever tell you how I met your father?" Mom asks us. Of course, Susannah and I have heard this story many times, but we are always happy to hear her tell us once again. So Susannah and I wait patiently as she starts to regale us with her story.

"It was when I lived in Birmingham, Michigan with my parents. It was 1982; I was twenty years old and still living at home. College was out of the question with my father's income, so after high school graduation, I began to work as a bank teller at a local bank and that is where I met my friend Sandy Sherman, who also was a bank teller. She couldn't believe that I didn't have a boyfriend, and she kept wanting to set me up with her friend, John Bennett. As you know, nobody in their right mind likes blind dates, but to make it less nerve-wracking Sandy told me that she and her boyfriend would tag along, too." She stops a moment to take a sip of coffee and then continues.

"Sandy told me to meet them at a sleazy bar just down the street from our workplace in downtown Birmingham. When I walked into the bar, the lights were non-existent, and I couldn't see my fingers through the cigarette smoke-hazed darkness. But, suddenly, I felt this strong firm grip on my arm, and standing in front of me was the most handsome man I have ever seen. I mean movie-star quality like Rhett Butler in *Gone with the Wind*. He was very tall, with short-cropped dark brown hair, and he had these hypnotizing vivid green eyes.

I thought to myself, *This must be John*, and I became very excited about our blind date. It was "Love at First Sight" for me. But then I was startled out of my infatuated stupor when I heard Sandy's voice, "Over here, Rose. I see you have met my boyfriend, Frank Spencer. If I was sitting in a chair, I believe I would have fallen off." She laughs.

"I had to quickly regroup and pretend I didn't sense this attraction toward Frank. I met my blind date John and although he was a nice enough guy, he wasn't Frank. All night I couldn't stop myself from watching Frank's every move. Several times I even caught him staring at me, too." This time, my mom giggles. "When he asked me to dance, I too eagerly said yes. The look Sandy gave me should have singed my eyebrows, but I took his hand and proudly walked out on the dance floor anyways."

"And that was how we met. He broke up with Sandy that night and called me the next day. Of course, I may have lost a friend, but what I gained was so much more. There was no way I was going to live my life without Frank, and we got married six months later. But what makes me sad to this very day is that he promised to stay with me forever. I wish he didn't leave me so soon. I wasn't ready to say goodbye."

Reaching for the box of tissues on the counter, and handing one to my sister and mother, I say, "You are right, Mom. Susannah and I weren't either." And we all hug.

When our parents first met, my dad, at the age of 27, had just graduated from Eastern Michigan University's School of Fire; followed by completion of the Fire Fighter Training Division at Wayne County Community College. My father's decision to become a firefighter had much to do with his muscular physique and his fearlessness. He was a proud and powerful man who wanted to do something useful with his physical strength. His 6'4" stature, compounded with the fact that he weighed 230 pounds, proved to be an impressive asset in his career choice.

However, with much dismay from newlywed Rose, Frank wanted to become a firefighter in one of the most prestigious fire departments in the country, the New York Fire Department. And they began to build their married life on Long Island. In the beginning, with the unorthodox hours of a firefighter, 36 hours on and 24 hours off, it was very hard for Rose to adapt to her new surroundings, especially since she had no friends and family nearby.

It wasn't until the birth of my sister and then myself, followed by the twins, that my mother began to enjoy living in the state of New York.

Chapter 2

"But, I really can't go on accepting gifts from you, though you are awfully kind." I read with what I thought was my Scarlett O'Hara southern belle drawl.

"I'm not kind. I'm just tempting you," my mom Rose speaks in a manly nasal manner. *"I never give anything without expecting something in return. I always get paid."*

"If you think I'll marry you to pay for the bonnet, I won't."
"Don't flatter yourself. I'm not a marrying man."
"Well, I won't kiss you for it either."
"Open your eyes and look at me. No, I don't think I will kiss you... although you need kissing badly. That's what's wrong with you. You should be kissed and often. And by someone who knows how."

My mom and I were passing a worn, but beloved book of *Gone with the Wind* back and forth.

"Oh, and I suppose you think you're the proper person."
"I might be if the right moment ever came."
"You're a conceited, black-hearted varmint Rhett Butler. And I don't know why I let you come and see me."
"I'll tell you why, Scarlett. Because I'm the only man over 16 and under 60... who's around to show you a good time."
"But cheer up, the war can't last much longer."
"Oh really, Rhett? Why?"
"There's a battle going on right now that ought to pretty well fix things... one way or the other."
"Oh, Rhett. Is Ashley in it?"

"You still haven't gotten the wooden-headed Mr. Wilkes out of your mind. Yes, I suppose he's in it."

"Oh, but tell me, Rhett, where is it?"

"Some little town in Pennsylvania called Gettysburg."

My mother and I are thoroughly enjoying our reading enactment of *Gone with the Wind* sitting in the white thatched gazebo in my sister's secret garden oasis backyard when we suddenly hear a male deep-throated voice, yelling 'Bravo, bravo' and the sound of clapping hands.

Flustered by the intrusion, I yell back, "Will the eavesdropper please show his presence?"

When a man's head and torso appear above the ivy-covered block wall separating my sister's backyard from the home adjacent to hers, I can't help but scream, "Not only are you an eavesdropper, but also you are a peeping, Tom, too."

Chuckling, he responds, "You are very quick with the accusations. You asked for me to show myself, so I did. But perhaps you should just put the handcuffs on me right now," reaching out both of his hands, he continues speaking. "I just overheard, not eavesdropped, your reading of one of my mother's favorite movies. I have seen that movie so many times, I could quote just about every line. Plus, I was enchanted by your southern accent, but now I realize that was just a fraud."

"Ha," I say, "You think you are funny, but you should mind your own business."

"Perhaps you are right." Scratching behind his right ear. He bows and simultaneously says, "Excuse me ladies for interrupting your beautiful day." And then he disappears from our view.

When I turn toward my mother to make a crude comment, I notice my sister holding a tray with three glasses of lemonade standing inside the gazebo with a look of unbelievable shock on her face.

"Do you know who that is?" Susannah asks me.

"Don't tell me he is a famous actor. You know how bad I am with celebrity recognition. Although he does look vaguely familiar."

"No, he is not a famous actor. But have you ever seen the reality television show, "Love at First Sight"?"

Squirming in my seat, I respond, "I have not."

"Well, he is one of the eligible bachelors. This season they chose this up-and-coming neighborhood of Marina Del Rey, called Silicon Beach as their on-site location. Six bachelors live in that house which is adjacent to mine, and the bachelorettes live on the other side of the Bachelors' house."

Shrugging, I say, "Why didn't you warn me? I know I acted very rude, but that man deserved it, don't you think?"

"Sorry, I only caught the tail end of your conversation, so I cannot say." "Well," my mom adds, "Although he did interrupt our tranquil afternoon, I thought he had very nice manners."

"I suppose so, but I still think it was rude for him to eavesdrop, and I am glad I told him so. We didn't introduce ourselves, do you know what his name is Susannah?"

"I believe his name is Marcus, age 27, former law student... Not sure of anything else. At least that is what the caption reads whenever he is on camera. The first time I saw him on the show was when Marcus confided to his bachelorette date about his first sexual encounter. I thought he was quite a handsome man, with stunningly laser blue eyes that appeared to look right through the bachelorette, Amanda, 27, unemployed. Noticeably nervous about this confession, he had this charming habit of scratching behind his ear as he tried to tell this beautiful red-headed life-size Barbie doll about a very private matter.

He began to divulge the story about his first experience at 16 when he tried to have sex with his then high school girlfriend. He says that she didn't want to touch his penis, and he had to navigate his penis into her vagina, but he really wasn't sure where to put it either. He says it turned out to be a disastrous attempt, neither of them sure if that first try was even considered sex. After finishing his story, he managed to bestow upon the bachelorette, a seductive, lopsided smile revealing two provocative dimples, and said, "I've gotten much better with my navigation skills. I thought he was adorable, and now you have managed to have quite an impression on him."

"I did not and what I don't understand, though, is why someone would need to rely on a television show to fall in love. And the fact that they don't even get to make the final choice, would not appeal to me, either. As a writer, my curiosity is definitely piqued."

Handing us each a lemonade and then sitting down on one of the comfy cushions next to my mom, my sister continues, "I believe that some people go on these shows for several reasons. One, to supposedly fall in love. Two to become noticed celebrity-wise through social media, and three, just for kicks. My favorite part of watching these shows is to categorize each of the bachelors and bachelorettes into each of these groups. It's trying to figure out who is who that makes the show interesting to me. As for Marcus, I haven't figured him out yet, but it is only two weeks into the season."

We continue reading the book that entire afternoon, with much laughter, until we hear Alex call out our names, dinner forgotten but precious memories definitely preserved. Absently, we overlooked the fact that today is the maid's day off. Pizza will have to do.

Waking up the next morning in the guest bedroom which I have designated entirely as my own, I realize that due to the three-hour time change, it is early. Anxious to start my day, I pull on comfortable sweatpants, an old T-shirt, and tennis shoes. Knowing that no one else will be awake, I grab my computer and my cell phone and sneak out the back door to the gazebo, so I could collect my sleepy cob-webbed thoughts and then call my office back in New York knowing their wheels have been churning for hours. The waves crashing onto the sandy shore create the only sound in this early morning solitude, where even the sun has barely made its appearance behind the scatter of clouds.

An hour into my solitude, I am surprised when Susannah comes bouncing out fully dressed in a flowing yellow maxi dress toting two cups of steamy coffee. She hands me mine, with just the right amount of cream. Knowing how she savors her sleep, I look up at her quizzically.

"I couldn't sleep. Today is a very exciting day for me. I have scheduled an ultrasound for this morning, you and Mom get to join Alex and me to get a sneak peek at our baby." Susannah's face glows from the pure pleasure of going on this adventure.

Reaching the doctor's office, Alex has already arrived, so we are ushered immediately into an exam room to begin the procedure. Alex holds onto one of Susannah's hands. At first, the doctor chats away, commenting on the healthy heartbeat, perfect head measurements, and the estimated due date, and then suddenly, she becomes quiet which alarms Susannah.

"Is something wrong, Dr. Hannah?"

Realizing her mistake, the doctor quickly smiles and says, "Oh no, no, everything is fine. But, if you are interested in knowing if this baby is a girl or boy, I am 99% sure of its gender."

Susannah glances at Alex, and immediately makes a decision without waiting for his response. "Yes, we want to know right now. I do not want to decorate the baby's room with generic yellow and green wallpaper."

"Well, then," the nurse continues, "I think you will be delighted to know you can decorate the nursery with pink and white accents."

At first, it didn't register, but suddenly Susannah's face lights up, and she claps her hands, "It's a girl, Alex. I just knew it."

Alex, smiling, bends down to give Susannah a soft kiss on the lips and murmurs, "I hope she looks just like her mother and her grandmother." The look in my sister's eyes is priceless. Susannah is an exact replica of my mother with their blond hair, pale skin, blue eyes, and petite form.

Excited, Susannah gazes at our mom and says, "Now is a good time to let you know the name we had picked out if the baby is a girl. Francesca Rose, Frankie for short."

And my mom begins to cry. Pulling herself together, she softly says, "I am honored and so is your father. Will you please remember to tell Frankie Rose that Grandma Rose fell in love with her the first time I laid my eyes on her inside her mommy's belly? It is love at first sight."

"Mom," Susannah says quickly, "You can tell her yourself on the day she is born when you hold her in your arms."

"Honey, you know that is not going to happen."

All three of us are shocked by her statement. None of us know what to say, so we don't say anything. As mentioned before, my mom has terminal lung cancer, and her life expectancy is somewhere between four and six months. She has always been a fighter and usually doesn't give up so easily. Her response gives me a very sad reality check.

Chapter 3

Marcus, 27, Former Law Student

As the only son of prominent and celebrity-known news personalities, one would think that I was born with an iconic silver spoon in my mouth. But think the opposite. My parents met each other when they were both money-hungry, nobodies driven by the need to be somebody. My mother was a weather girl and my father had just been hired by the same local television network as a local news reporter. It took long, exhausting years of commitment and dedication for them to become the well-known news anchors they are today.

When I was old enough to understand, they sat me down and drilled into me the fact that success requires diligence and perseverance and that they would expect no less from me. My choice to go to law school was not a surprise to them, but an expected decision on my part to meet their preconceived expectations.

After two and a half years of spending every single hour of my extremely studious life as a law student inside the Loyola Law Library, I can't wait to have fun! The only consistent break I take during those long and laborious months in law school happens every Thursday night at 9:00 pm watching "Love at First Sight" with five other male law students, Peter, David, Conner, Aaron, and Blake. The show becomes our anchor to reality, but nowhere near what you would call normalcy. Peter, one of the nerdiest guys I know, is a master at computer technology so he designed a detailed fantasy program for "Love at First Sight". Each week, the six of us voted on who will get the first kiss, who will have the most embarrassing on-air debacle and even down to who is matched up at the end of the season.

For the two last seasons of "Love at First Sight," my ability to pick who would be matched up with who has won me… four bottles of stale, off-brand tequila, and a three-month subscription to Playboy Magazine. None of us have much money, so our reward prizes are lacking in substance, except for the

Playboy Magazine subscription that my buddy Peter donated to the winning pot. Peter is highly competitive, and his motive for giving away that subscription is to provide himself with an advantage when finals come around, hoping that my studying will be preempted by the nude photos. Unfortunately for him and lucky for me, he doesn't realize that the subscription does not have an expiration date, which means I can activate it anytime, which I speedily did once my finals were over.

After we have finished law school, our next imminent task is to study for the law bar exams. I can't really admit which was worse, studying for the bar or taking it. But I am overjoyed to have gotten this far in my studies.

Based on our high LSAT scores upon entry into Loyola Law School, a select few have been chosen as participants by the law school to complete our law school studies in two and a half years instead of three. There are 50 of us picked, and that is how I met Peter, Aaron, Blake, Connor, and David.

One of the advantages of finishing law school in this shorter time is that we get to graduate in December, and then cram for the bar exam which we take in February. Other students at Loyola Law School will graduate the following May and take the bar exam in July.

The disadvantage is that we are taking on a heavier load each semester. Not sure if we were the lucky chosen or just plain guinea pigs.

After taking the bar exam, our brains, completely over-used and now under-stimulated, hunger for a much-needed releasable outlet before each of us undertakes the long and tedious hours at our chosen prestigious law firms. I will be working for Turner and Copeland Entertainment, a company where I did my first internship and who at the time offered me a position once I passed the bar.

However, it is during one of these deprived moments after taking the bar and feeling as if our brains have been turned inside out, that the six of us decided to audition for the show, "Love at First Sight" for laughs. None of us are currently attached, so we thought why not. Ironically, I am the first to notice that the acronym for the show is LAFS.

Unfortunately, and with much regret, I am the only one selected for this season. My first obstacle is to inform Turner and Copeland Entertainment that I will not be able to start working for them on the agreed-upon date. Thank goodness, they understand, but I am sure they were surprised by my announcement and wondered why I am doing this reality show.

And even more disconcerting, is something I keep asking myself, "Why am I doing this?" That is a good question, and I do not have an intelligent answer except I am overdue for just plain fun. Do I want to fall in love? Of course. Will I find love on this show where that choice is totally out of my control? Not sure, but I am willing to try since my past relationships have not worked out well.

I met my only long-time girlfriend Kelsey during my junior year of undergraduate school at the University of Southern California. We decided to live together after we both graduated from USC, and I began my first year at Loyola Law School in Los Angeles. My priorities changed, and our relationship began to decline from there. I can still hear her thin, tinny, whiny voice every time I return home from my day filled with law classes, followed by copious hours in the law library.

"Marcus, why didn't you call me? I made your favorite chicken dinner and now it is ruined." I think she only knew how to cook chicken because I can't remember her making anything else.

Trying to console her, I reply, "Kelsey, how many times do I have to tell you not to wait up for me, not to plan any meals, and to socialize with your friends after work." Kelsey, an intelligent person, graduated with a marketing business degree and was hired by Target in their marketing department in downtown Los Angeles. She had many opportunities to branch out and meet up with friends, but these annoying conversations continue on a weekly basis until I finally told her to move out just before I finished my first year of law school. After that failed relationship, I dabble a little bit in online dating during summer internships because, one, I had the time and, two, I was lonely.

The concept of online dating is not exactly what it sounds like. Once you choose a particular online dating site, believe me, there are too many to mention, you must complete a profile about yourself. This is the tricky part. Do you divulge every aspect of your life, do you exaggerate, or just put the plain, dull facts and wait to tell the selected matched date about yourself? I chose to be direct, simple, and uncomplicated.

I listed my age, my profession (law student), and a few facts about my likes and dislikes. When I am asked about the perfect date, I just wrote: "No drama." But most important and above all else when completing your profile are the photos that you must submit. I downloaded a ridiculous selfie and a photo of myself sitting in the law library studying... simple and true.

Within a day, I received four notifications that I have matched. This is when it gets a little aggravating to be on these sites. Three of the matches were definitely not my type, as I immediately surmised after looking at their photo. But one of the matches piqued my interest. She sent me a wave and texted that she would love to meet me for coffee. My first instinct was to check out her profile since it was obvious she has looked at mine.

Opening up her profile, I am surprised to see a variety of attractive photos of this girl in her mid-20s. Her profile stated that she is 'looking for love'. She lived in Los Angeles and worked as an executive assistant at a downtown law firm. *Great,* I thought, *we might have something in common.* So I texted her back, and we made plans to meet at a Starbucks coffee shop convenient for both of us. She informed me her name is Sharon.

When I walked into Starbucks, I noticed three women seated alone at tables. They all had dark auburn hair like Sharon's, but none of them resembled the photo in the profile. One of the girls was dressed very masculine, with a black tank top and tight black jeans that accentuated her huge belly protruding over her low-rise jeans. Now Sharon's profile stated that she had a slim build, so I discounted the girl in black.

The next girl, very tall and straight, has a slim build with a flowery sun dress exposing her bony shoulders. Now this could be Sharon, but before I made a fool of myself, I now address the third girl. She had her back to me, so in order to see her more clearly, I walked over to the register to order a drink. I notice that girl number three was on her cell phone, and when I heard a loud, throaty laughter, I couldn't help but turn my head toward her.

The laugh was so authentically, the most beautiful sound I have ever heard. And then I took a double-take look at her face, and I am astounded by the breathtaking beauty of this woman. *Please let it be her,* I told myself. I checked my phone and brought up her profile on the dating app, and realized it was her. Now that I have convinced myself, that it was her, I built up the courage to walk over to where she was sitting.

"Sharon?" I ask.

Slowly, she stood up, smiled, and reached out her surprisingly warm, large hand and shook mine with a very strong grip. "Yes, nice to meet you, Marcus." Why was I surprised that the sexy, deep voice resounding from her throat matched her laugh?

We sat at her table, after ordering our lattes, and talked for over three hours. I found out she was an only child like me, and that she actually wanted to be a lawyer and was trying to save money to apply to law schools. She is ambitious, funny, and very intelligent, and I enjoyed our time together. We agreed to have dinner next weekend and exchanged cell phone numbers.

Throughout the week, we texted each other on a daily basis, still trying to learn as much about each other as possible. It was very exciting during this discovery period since she was a very captivating and clever conversational texter, and I am looked forward to our date.

By the time Saturday night came around, I couldn't wait to see her again. We met at the restaurant, and I felt a sense of pride to have her walking beside me, noticing the envious looks of the male patrons. I believe her height must be around 5'11 since she almost reached my eye level. The dinner was lovely, and the chemistry between us was obvious. As our time together was nearing the end, I couldn't wait to put my arms around her and kiss her lush, red lips.

She had this way of pouting in a very seductive manner, which turned me on, no doubt. At the end of the evening, I walked her to her car, and I couldn't resist pulling her into my arms. With no hesitation, my lips seeked hers, deepening into an intimate heat, scorching kiss.

She wraped her arms around my neck, pressing her warm, hard body against mine. I sucked in my breath at the contact. Passion, too long suppressed, exploded as our mouths continued to search, a throaty moan escaped her lips. When we parted, we were both breathless, wonderment at the physical connection between us.

Later that night as I laid in bed, I have a strong sense of satisfaction knowing that I had just met a very incredible, special lady and look forward to seeing this relationship grow. Just about to close my eyes, I felt the vibration of an incoming call on my cell phone. My heart skipped a beat when I realized it was Sharon.

Picking up immediately, "Hi, sexy, do you miss me, too?"

"Yes, I actually do. I can't seem to fall asleep because you are sooooo on my mind."

"Ditto."

"Marcus, can I ask you a question? Especially after tonight's fireworks between us, and before we allow this relationship to progress any further, I believe in transparency. And, besides, your answer is very important."

Not sure where this conversation was going, I immediately jumped in, "No, I am not married, if that is what you are asking?"

"Good to know, but that is not the question." Hesitating momentarily, she spurted out, "Are you bisexual?"

I had just taken a drink from my water bottle, and when she asked me that question, I spit out the entire contents.

"No, and why would you be asking me that? I like women and only women. I am sure from that kiss we had tonight, it is very obvious, right?"

"Well, I wasn't sure because I am bisexual, and I am a transvestite. I am actually a man, with all the essential parts."

Now, I was confused by this confession. "Wait, you are a guy. How can that be? You are such a beautiful woman. I have never met a guy or girl who is as strikingly beautiful as you are."

"I was hoping that gender didn't matter to you. We definitely have a physical attraction, regardless of whether or not we are both men. Are you open to this type of relationship, Marcus?"

Stunned by her revelation, I answered, "Hell no! I am sorry Sharon, but this type of arrangement is not acceptable to my conservative, stodgy background." And to think that I kissed a man with such passion, really turned my stomach inside out. After we hung up, the first thing I chose to do was rush to the bathroom and vomit into the toilet, followed by brushing my teeth, scrubbing my lips until they were raw, and then gargling with mouthwash.

When I woke up in the morning, I realized I may have overreacted to Sharon's confession, and it wasn't necessary for me to be sick over the situation. I am not against transvestites or bisexuality, it is just not my thing.

But this one encounter totally destroyed my quest in online dating. And now here I am, on a reality television show desperately looking for love.

Chapter 4

Marcus, 27, Former Law Student

My encounters with the six chosen bachelorettes can be described as insightful. I find it perplexing and tiresome to talk to each of the bachelorettes whenever we have group dates which consist of all twelve of us getting together. Due credit is given to the creators of this show since they have been able to schedule a variety of unique opportunities for these group dates—cooking lessons, pool parties, cocktail parties, spa days, and the most interesting so far, karate lessons. Mind you, all of the bachelors are trying to impress the ladies, so you can imagine the macho-invested antics overflowing in abundance.

And what more can I say about the incredibly gorgeous and overzealous group of too-perfect, possibly underachieving women? Most of them probably have never read a book cover to cover, except for one of those smut entertainment magazines. Of course, I haven't been able to dissect and analyze each woman, but that is just my general impression.

Cheyenne, my first one-on-one date is beyond gorgeous. Native American, her naturally straight blue-black hair flowing down her back, her subtle honey brown skin, her Hershey chocolate almond-shaped eyes, can make a man lose his identity. The only fault I detect in this calm, collected woman is her inability to adapt to the egotistical aggressiveness of a man's world. Shy and reserved, she speaks without giving direct eye contact as though she questions her own actions unlike the other bachelorettes on the show who can be described as over-assertive and secure. Neither are my type, but I have to keep my options open.

"Cheyenne, tell me a little about yourself," I ask as we are being escorted by a hostess to our private table on top of the roof of the Four Seasons Resort in Santa Barbara. Sparing no costs, our first date consisted of an incredible Pacific Ocean view-filled helicopter ride from Marina Del Rey to Santa Barbara.

Cheyenne exhibits qualities unlike any other woman I have met before. When she tells me that she was raised on an Indian Reservation, I am not surprised. "My parents died when I was young, so I was sent to an Indian Reservation to live with my grandmother. I lived a very secluded life in Montana until I turned 18. At that time, I attended UCLA undergraduate school. I am currently in their graduate program in Design and Media Arts and hope to pursue a career in film editing."

"Have you ever been in love before?" I ask, hoping to create a more personal connection with her.

"No," she speaks in her soft, quiet voice, "That was not one of my priorities until now. I would love to fall in love and get married. I never had a close relationship with my parents or even my grandmother, for that matter. I intend to find a soulmate who will be my best friend, my lover, and my confidante. Someone who I can trust deeply, and someone who loves me as much as I love them."

"Cheyenne, I think you deserve to find that person. All those qualities that you listed are definitely what I would want for myself." Satisfied that she felt comfortable enough to share her most precious thoughts, I continue to share tidbits about myself, too. By the end of the evening, both of us sense a mutual admiration for each other. As I lean over to kiss her soft, inviting lips, Cheyenne seems just as eager for the contact.

This brings me to my second one-on-one date, Amanda, who reminds me of the hare-brained rabbit from the ever-ready battery commercial. Needy and pushy, she speaks non-stop with a territorial voice, insisting that we talk about our first sexual encounters, which I reluctantly spill. Tall with piercing green eyes and reddish-blonde hair, it was impossible to give her my full attention as I kept imagining her long legs wrapped around my own waist. Unlike my first one-on-one date, the kiss at the end of the night was expected from this very eager girl.

This Sunday afternoon, the show is airing a scheduled group fun day, a pool party, and barbeque. Ready for the rigorous challenge, I plan to flirt mercilessly with the other four bachelorettes. I will use this unique opportunity to narrow down my options and make sure the live audience tunes into which bachelorette would be a good match for me. It would be undoubtedly amazing to find a real girlfriend after the season ends.

The only imminent drawback of being selected as one of the eligible bachelors is the fact that I am 'signed, sealed, and delivered' and honor-bound to have no contact with the outside world. Our personal belongings were thoroughly searched once we arrived on the premises... no cell phones, no computers. Since none of my best buddies were selected, I wish I could come up with a fool-proof way to get their undeniably needed input. Undoubtedly, I do not have any remotely common interests with many of the men in the house. Most of the men exhibit a cocky, chauvinist demeanor similar to that of a crude and ill-mannered primitive caveman which has created consistent, laughable banter throughout the bachelor house.

A few of us who have a brain worth using have been labeled the 'brainiacs' which are me, Jack, 25, a real estate broker, and Dusty, 26, a medical intern. To take no offense, we refer to the rest of them as the 'macho-boys', Damon, 27, aspiring actor; Noah, 29, Bar Owner; and Kevin, 28, bodybuilder. Normally, I don't have a problem adapting and blending in, but sometimes I feel the need to escape the clown-like, childish behavior displayed on a daily basis by the 'boys'. Which brings me to my first mistake on the show.

Two weeks into the "Love at First Sight" season, wallowing in the cool Santa Ana breeze in the blooming rose gardens beyond the pool house, hoping to escape the testosterone-filled 'bachelor pad' on a late March afternoon, I overheard a conversation I deeply regret. I was caught red-handed eavesdropping on the neighbor to the left of our house rehearsing one of my favorite scenes from *Gone with the Wind*.

Rhett Butler, one of the main characters in the book, has just presented Scarlett O'Hara with a lovely new bonnet. Understand that this scene is during the Civil War, and new bonnets as well as any type of luxury, are forbidden. However, it is the light-hearted flirtation and taunting tone of Rhett that makes this scene special. I know I shouldn't have made myself known, but the enchanting southern drawl of one of the women reciting the lines made me forget my manners. In the future, I will be more careful with my elusive escapades so as not to interfere with another's peaceful afternoon, in addition to breaching the show's privacy contract.

Chapter 5

Rina, 27, Freelance Writer

Acute curiosity has always been one of my worst qualities. That is why I became a reporter by day and writer at night. So, ever since that accidental meeting with the bachelor Marcus, I am anxious to hear his side of the story of why he chooses to be on this reality show. Based on my initial observation, he is not bad-looking, possibly resembling a younger George Clooney, so finding girls with those good looks should not be a deterrent for him. Which makes me wonder even more why he is on this show.

Lucky for me, my current job allows me to write articles on any subject of interest so long as it deals with food, fashion, entertainment, and travel. So really the sky is the limit. My last article dissected the latest fad... the notoriety of trendy green kale versus old-fashioned iceberg lettuce, in the past few years. Nowadays, I can't walk into a restaurant, a grocery store, or even a farmer's market without noticing the popularity of kale-inspired choices or recipes such as kale martinis. Several years ago, kale was not even a word in anybody's daily vocabulary.

So, obviously, trendy subjects will continue to be of interest to the general public, which is why I am definitely intrigued about this reality show, "Love at First Sight". But, for now, I am doing some research on the pros and cons for United States citizens to travel to Cuba. As of January 15, 2015, United States citizens can now travel to Cuba once again. That is why Cuba, a very beautiful Caribbean Island, is now considered one of the most desirable and obscure destinations of the year.

***

It's not every day that one lives next door to the taping of an atypical reality program which is the reason I am snooping around my sister's backyard hoping to catch a glance of Marcus or even one of the other bachelors. Susannah's backyard is beyond gorgeous. Beginning with the infinity pool which creates an image of flowing into the Pacific Ocean, to the immaculately maintained vegetable garden sprouting ripe, red tomatoes and leafy greens, to the secret garden surrounded by blooming vines, palm trees, and assorted wildflowers. This is where the gazebo sits and where I had my first encounter with Marcus.

It is late in the afternoon and if I listen closely, I can hear the faint sounds of splashing mingled with male and female laughter. Attuned to any new sounds, I am surprised to catch a few words from some whispered conversations coming closer to the point that I didn't have to guess what they were saying.

"Oh, Marcus, ever since I saw you that first night, I had hoped that you would seek me out. Tell me about yourself."

"Well, Lisa, that is your name, right?"

Giggling, "Yes, but my close friends call me Lees, and I hope I can consider you one of my close friends."

I gasp when she says that and then immediately realize that they may have heard me. Not wanting to get caught eavesdropping, I rush to the gazebo, and I try to make myself invisible while concentrating on emails on my computer. Thankfully, the voices fade into the night.

A few minutes later, startling me out of my stupor, I am rudely interrupted by a voice telling me that 'the pot sure is calling the kettle black'.

Searching for the unidentified voice, knowing full well who it belongs to, I am not surprised when Marcus pops up from his usual spot, revealing a mocking grin.

Pretending that I don't know what he is referring to, I say, "I don't know what you are talking about. Why don't you mind your own business?"

"I would like to do that, but just for once, stop with the contradictory denials, and let's call it even, okay. Maybe we should design a schedule so that we won't be occupying the same space at the same time."

"How would we do that since we happen to live side by side, and you seem to enjoy encroaching into my solitude."

"Come on, you know that isn't the case. You were eavesdropping on my conversation, too."

Surprisingly, I find myself enjoying this playful banter but realize that perhaps we should come up with a plan. "Listen, Mister... what is your name by the way?"

"My name is Marcus Granger and how should I address you?"

"My name is Katerina Spencer, but my close friends call me Rina," accentuating the last word. And then we both laugh, instantly breaking the ice.

"Nice to see you do have a sense of humor, Miss Spencer."

"Yes, actually I do. Let's make a deal, Marcus. First, I will try my best not to listen to your private and most intimate conversations as long as you reciprocate. Second, if ever you need to talk to someone from the outside world, seek me out, and we can talk."

"I can't do that. I signed a contract promising to avoid contact with the outside world. If I get caught," his eyes hold a sparkle to them and a duplicate pair of sexy dimples expose themselves, "I could be asked to leave."

"We can't have that happen, can we? How else will you fall in "Love at First Sight"?"

"Touche," he laughs.

"I understand all that legal nonsense, but what if we become friends and talk about mundane things that have nothing to do with the show? It seems as though you are always seeking solitude, and I enjoy my alone time, too." There is no way I will let him know I am a writer. I want him to think that I am a person of no interest before I let him know my ulterior motive.

"Well, Miss Spencer I better get back to my duties as an enraptured bachelor looking for love. Until we meet again."

Smiling, I can't help but ask. "Marcus, what is it you are standing on? I have seen you on the show, and know that you are not eight feet tall."

Chuckling, he says, "No, I am not that tall, but this handy wrought iron bench adds a few feet to my normal average height." And, with that said, he disappears.

Turning my attention back to my computer, I am pleased to hear my FaceTime ring and see two smiling faces looking back at me. "Well," I say, "If it isn't the two traveling vagabonds, Dr. Jekyll and Mr. Hyde. So glad you two can take a minute out of your busy schedules to call and see how your mother is doing."

"Oh, come on, Rina," Randall, the more vocal twin pipes in. "You know we had this European cruise scheduled way before Mom's diagnosis. We have booked our flights for SoCal and will be there in two weeks."

"Good, Mom keeps asking about you both."

My twin brothers, Scott and Randall, are as different as night and day. Scott is gay and Randall is not. Scott is taller than Randall by a good three inches, declares himself a vegan, and is overly thin, quiet, and soft-spoken. He lives with his life partner, Chuck, whom he met at the accounting firm, Benson and Hallows, where they are both employed.

Randall looks and acts exactly like my dad, Frank, and has followed in his footsteps as a firefighter. Thick and muscular, loud and boisterous, Randall's crudeness has made it difficult for him to find the right girl which is always a conversation he wants to avoid while visiting our mom. Her repetitive questions create much friction between the two of them, "So, Randall, when are you finally going to meet a nice girl and settle down?"

He considers himself a funny man, and always comes back with, "It's hard to be serious with girls I consider the flavor of the month." This shuts my mom up quickly. But Randall is just like a big teddy bear waiting for someone to pick him up and hold him. He has always used his jokes and laughter to cover up the void of not having a father figure around.

It was not easy for my brothers to grow up without the much-needed influence of our father. They never knew what family ties are all about. They don't remember the Sunday family outings, beach vacations, or the simple act of eating dinner together for every meal. Left alone with only each other after school for most of their prepubescent years, while my mom either worked or attended nursing classes and my sister, and I tried to deal with our own loss, they learned to rely on each other for everything.

This cemented their relationship to the point that it ultimately, and sadly, excluded my sister and me from being principal role players in their lives. I love my brothers, and I would do anything for them, but I know deep down in my heart that I would be the last person either of them would approach in an emergency. And, if I ever have one wish, I would go back in time and give those little boys the love and care they needed.

Understand that when my father died, the US Congress immediately created the 11th Victim Compensation Fund for the fallen victims and my mother received over two million dollars, so money was not an issue. My mom spoiled all of us, but extravagant gifts were not what we needed.

September 11 changed the entire context of our family. My mom's soulful dedication to finding my father following that fateful day occupied her only thoughts. Immediately after September 11, her daily heartbreaking schedule began with dropping the four of us at school. She would take a taxi as close to Ground Zero as possible. Then she would walk the rest of the way, sometimes 3–5 miles, and join in with the rescue and search teams.

She refused to believe that my father was dead, but after two weeks, she realized that there is no way he could have survived, but she still chose to be there.

Our thoughtful and dear neighbors set up a daily dinner schedule so that we never went without a homemade cooked meal at dinner time. Another neighbor, who had a boy the same age as the twins, wholeheartedly picked up my brothers after school, and fed and kept them until bedtime. This terrorist event changed the history of my life, the cities, and the nation. Strangers came together and helped one another. It was a sad time and an amazing time.

Every day, my mother came home at dusk, zombielike, her clothes covered in ash and soot, her fingers bloody and cut, her hair dirty, charred, and matted down. My sister and I would draw a bath for her and gently ease her into the bathtub fully clothed, undress her, and try to remove some of the grime from her sallow-looking skin. Once we saw some semblance of life return to her eyes, we would dress her in a comfy cotton nightgown, tuck her into bed, and try to get her to eat some of the leftover casseroles. Then we would bring the boys in to say good night to her. Each of them sat on one side of my mom, vying for attention that she could not give. We did this nightly for almost two months.

One thing I am grateful for is that I am so glad that we sheltered the boys and did not let them glimpse the heartbreaking shell of their mother those first two months because I know how her distraught image is ingrained in my brain and how it affected who I am today. I can only imagine what it would have done to the young sponge-like minds of my brothers.

After two months of searching for any remains of my father, my mother woke up one morning and decided that change was in order. Everyone deals with grief in different ways, and her incredible journey is living proof. She decided to give back to the community that gave so much to her and enrolled in nursing school. Nursing school consumed her days and when she didn't have any classes, she would volunteer at the local hospitals where she thrived as a caregiver for others.

Our lives returned to as near normal as could be expected. Dinnertime came to be an important part of our lives, in which communication was the key element. She wanted to hear every detail of our lives, and she gave each of us her full attention. It was as if she was trying to make up for the last two months. I know her guilt lies with her abandonment during that time and since then she has always tried to make up for that.

In the end, she came to realize that material items did not make up for her absence, and we needed her. I am not sure how much my brothers remember her absence during that time, but I can guarantee that it molded who they are today... needy, insecure, independent, and downright selfish.

I am not surprised that before they hung up with our FaceTime session, they told me, "We are not sure how much money is left from the initial survivor's fund, but we all know that Mom's lung cancer is due to her exposure at Ground Zero during those first few weeks, and we think we should ask for more compensation."

I forewarned Susannah about the greed-infested nature of our brothers, and she will be furious with the twins when I fill her in on their intentions. Knowing full well they are only interested in how much they will inherit once our mother dies, I can't wait for their visit to watch the sparks fly when Susannah gets a hold of them.

My sister Susannah is a raging firecracker when it comes to any kind of selfish or self-absorbed behavior. Do not cross her. Believe me, I know from personal experience. Once when we were very young, I had this bad and ridiculous habit of pulling the hair out of my toy dolls.

And once and only once, I made the inexplicable mistake of confusing one of my dolls with Susannah's, and when she found her bald doll, she wrapped my entire body that night with glue and newspaper like a papier-mâché puppet while I was sleeping. I woke up and could not move. Never again will I upset my sister, and I think the boys are going to be in for a surprise when dealing with her.

Susannah is smart, unselfish, and the most generous person I know. She graduated from NYU with a business degree and then went to FIDM to learn all she could about home decorating. She had planned to start her own home decorating business, and when she sets her mind to anything, she succeeds. But, when she met Alex at her best friend Mira's wedding, everything changed.

Alex, second cousin to Mira, had flown into New York for the wedding, and when he met Susannah, they hit it off instantly, discussing home decorating ideas and the fact that he had just bought a new home in the new and upcoming area called Silicon Beach. Lucky for Alex, he became Susannah's first and only client.

But I am glad the twins will be here soon because my mom's health is rapidly declining. I am literally witnessing her body change from a bulimic-looking teenager to that of a bony skeleton. Her sleep habits have changed drastically, from seven hours at night to thirteen hours. Her appetite seems non-existent, picking at her food, unable to finish half of a sandwich or child-sized bowl of cereal. But ask her if she wants a bowl of ice cream—she never says no.

Hospice comes in twice a week to check her vitals and adjust pain medication as needed. They initiated a regimen of oxygen at night and the continuous sound of *swoosh, swoosh* resonates among the walls of the sleeping house at night.

Twice a week, Susannah and I bundle up our mom, as though we are going snowmobiling, for excursions such as the museum, the movies, or just a girl-talk lunch. We will do anything to solicit a smile from her all-too-thin lips. Lately, she has required the use of a walker, and sometimes a wheelchair to get around.

But this last outing with my mom had both Susannah and me in stitches. It was late one evening, and my mom was craving ice cream. Unfortunately, she had finished off the last carton of her favorite flavor, butter pecan the night before, and neither my sister nor I had the chance to pick up another carton today. We decided to go to the local ice cream shop.

We bundled Rose up in her winter parka and hat and buckled her up in the back seat. Not two minutes down the street, I looked back to check on Rose and noticed her sitting in the middle of the seat, not the right passenger side behind me. I started to laugh because she was sitting so straight in the seat with her knitted wool hat with a pom-pom on top, which reminded me of the crazy clown photo I once admired.

"Mom, you have to keep your seat belt on at all times. Please don't change seats while Susannah is driving." I reached back and buckled her back in.

Not four minutes later, I turned around, and now Rose was sitting behind Susannah on the left side of the car.

"Mom," I yell softly so as not to alarm Susannah while she is driving, "you have to stay seated and buckled up. Why are you moving from seat to seat?" Rose just looks at me with this smirk-like smile.

"Susannah, you have to pull over. I can't reach Mom to buckle her in." Susannah looks at me, rolling her eyes, both of us wondering what our mother is thinking.

We finally reach the ice cream store with no more seat changes, and I feel relieved.

After finishing our ice creams, we buckle Rose back in the back seat and head for home. Mind you, Rose hasn't spoken a word to either of us since we left the house, not even at the ice cream shop; Susannah and I are perplexed, to say the least.

Not two minutes away from the ice cream shop, I turn around, and I don't see Rose sitting in the seat we placed her in or any of the other seats.

"Mom, where are you?" Still no sound from Rose. Knowing she has to be back there somewhere, I unbuckle my seat belt and proceed to crawl into the back seat and there she is, lying in a ball behind my seat.

"Jesus, Mom, what are you doing down there?" Rose looked at me with a blank look on her face. Again, I had Susannah pull over. We both got out to help Rose back up, and when we lifted her out from behind my car seat, we saw a pile of torn tissue. Not just a small pile, it was an extreme amount of torn tissues the size of M&Ms.

And then we realized that Rose had been tearing the tissue the entire time while we were driving to and from the ice cream shop, and her changing seats was to prevent us from seeing what she was up to. Susannah and I looked at each other and started to laugh so hard, and we didn't stop laughing until we got home, and Rose continued to have this satisfied smug look on her face the entire drive home.

Susannah's last comment, "I should never have had that Kleenex box back there in the first place," only made Susannah and I laugh even harder.

***

As usual, my mother is taking a late afternoon nap, and tonight Susannah and Alex have made plans to meet up with friends for dinner, so I am left on my own once again. Seeking out my favorite place to relax, I am sitting in the gazebo with my computer, trying to come up with an interesting story for next month's issue. The sun is about to set over the ocean, and the view is breathtaking which is an intimidating distraction. Although I would love to surprise my boss with an article on reality television shows, I have not been able to figure out the appropriate angle that might interest our readers.

Every Thursday night since I arrived, me, my sister, and our mother watch "Love at First Sight".

I think I am more interested in seeing Marcus on the show than the show itself. He has this suave and confident way about him, but he is not over the top like some of the other bachelors. Not being impressed easily, I believe that some of the bachelorettes may be a good choice for him. Of course, they are all beautiful, but I can see that Marcus' interest lies with the women who are not too aggressive, easy to converse with, and those who like to have fun, without trying too hard. He seems to avoid those women who have a lecherous, territorial flirtatious manner about them.

I am tired of writing about the latest trends in food. This past month, after the 'kale' article, I wrote a sequel titled, "Move over kale, there is a new leaf on the branch." The Moringa tree leaves, grown in Haiti, Africa, and parts of Latin America have a unique nutritional content including high levels of calcium, potassium, protein, and vitamins A, B, C, D, and E. However, there is only one problem for the United States, shipping fresh leaves has become a deterrent, but I expect to see this product in some of the more specialty stores in the United States very soon. Writing an article that does not deal with food is high on my to-do list.

Every time I watch "Love at First Sight," I get this preconceived feeling that something isn't right. For instance, how can this show, in which the audience makes the final decision of who is matched with whom, have a success rate of 60%, whereas 'The Bachelor', which has been airing since 2002, has only a success rate of 11%. My sister and I have had several discussions regarding the differences between the reality shows focusing on love and decided to do some research comparing the three most popular reality shows, "Love at First Sight," 'The Bachelor', and 'The Bachelorette'.

In the reality show, 'The Bachelor', each season starts with 20-plus women vying for the attention of one bachelor for a period of seven weeks. At the end of this time frame, the bachelor must choose one woman to propose marriage. The average age of 'The Bachelor' on each season is 31 years old, and the height 6'1" Since the initiation of the show, it has been a success with eight million viewers, glued to the television. But the success rate is only 11%.

A sequel to 'The Bachelor', 'The Bachelorette' first aired in 2003. Each season lasts seven weeks beginning with one bachelorette and 20 plus men with the average age of the bachelorette of 26 years old. Not as popular as 'The Bachelor', 'The Bachelorette' was forced into a hiatus from 2005 to 2008. However, this show has a success rate of 30%, higher than 'The Bachelor', which means that 30% of the time, 'The Bachelorette' marries her chosen bachelor.

I realize that marriage accounts for the success rate of both 'The Bachelor' and 'The Bachelorette', whereas with "Love at First Sight," not so. Another major difference with "Love at First Sight" is that the show is taped live unlike the other two shows and each episode is immediately aired on television, with no editing or censoring. This aspect of the show makes it definitely more interesting to watch because the bloopers in this show are aired for all to see immediately.

More importantly and surprisingly, from what I can conclude, the success rate of "Love at First Sight" is based upon the audience choosing who is partnered with whom, with no accountability on whether or not the relationship lasts past three months. With that in mind, I can see where the success rate of the show would be much higher than that of either of the other two shows. I can't help but wonder how many of the couples are still together after the three-month period. I can only guess that the success rate of "Love at First Sight" would be much lower.

And regardless of the differences and similarities between all three reality shows, it is obvious that viewers just want to see couples fall in love and live happily ever after. And I see nothing wrong with that.

This week, Marcus had a date on a private yacht with a glossy dark-haired, blue-eyed girl named Katie, and I witnessed a change from his usually distant demeanor. His eyes held a distinct twinkle when he looked at her, and he gave her his unadulterated attention. Laughter came easily between the two of them, and I could tell that there was a chemical connection. For some reason that I was unsure of, I was hoping he wouldn't fall in love with anyone. I wanted him to come running to me and tell me about what a fraud the show is and how he felt duped at the same time. I need this story, but intriguing Katie could ruin my plans, and I do not like it.

Completely absorbed in my thoughts, I jump when Marcus yells out, "Hello, Miss Spencer."

My heart stops beating for a second. How is it possible for someone to sneak up on me so easily, especially when he is the one person I am deep in thought with? "Hi, Marcus, I see you escaped the masses again."

"Easily done. The cameras don't follow us around all day. They allow us some semblance of privacy. But we can't be meeting like this although I can't resist peeking over the wall to see if you are there. One day I am bound to get caught, and out I go."

"Come on," I gasped. "They wouldn't kick you off the show for accidentally talking to one of your neighbors. And, besides, we aren't doing anything illegal, just chatting about the weather."

"If we do get caught, just tell them that you don't watch the show and that you had no idea that I was one of the bachelors on a reality show."

Laughing, I say. "I can do that. But I must admit that I have started watching the show religiously ever since our first encounter. But, out of curiosity, can I ask a question about the interview process?"

Mocking me with raised eyebrows, he responds, "That depends."

Frowning, not wanting to be too serious, I continue, "Well, it is simple. For instance, do they do background checks on you to make sure that you are not a mass murderer or rapist? Do they ask you when your last relationship ended? Is there a time frame to be unattached before allowing you on the show? Just why were you selected?" I didn't intend to bombard him with all these questions, but I couldn't help myself.

"Some of those are loaded questions, and legally I am not sure if I can answer them, but I don't see the harm since you can probably get the answers on the internet these days. Of course, they do background checks on each of us. You cannot have a significant other when applying to be on the show and no, there is no timeframe as to when your last relationship was. Why was I chosen and not my friends? I ask myself that every day. But you must understand that the success of this show is based on ratings."

"Ratings coincide with audience participation. What does the audience want to see... drama, competition, quarrels, people falling in love? I believe I was chosen for one reason only, my notoriety as the son of celebrity-known newscasters. For some reason, people are interested in a peek into the lives of the child of someone famous, which in my case are my parents. But, of course, that is my opinion only."

"I didn't know that about your parents, how famous are they?"

Marcus' throat makes a deep, robust chuckling sound and says, "Probably not famous enough if you ask them. They are the primetime newscasters on KCWN."

"Aww, I get it. Perhaps you are right, Marcus. Maybe that is why you were selected, but at least it offers you the privileged opportunity to be on this show."

"Yeah, I guess so."

"And I truly appreciate your honesty. But what do you want out of your participation? You tell me that you interviewed for the show just for laughs, but finding true love, really? How can you let the audience choose who you should end up with? I don't understand the success rate of this show, and I can't fathom why anyone with half a brain would agree to go on this show."

"Then it's a good thing that you aren't on this show since it is obvious that you don't believe in letting things happen and just going with the flow. Do you ever have fun, Rina? And what about your personal life? Have you ever been in love? Or do you just pine your days away sitting in this gazebo, thinking up ways to attack my personal choices?"

When he finishes with his childish tirade, my hands are clenching and unclenching, and I am angry at his hurtful words. I jump up until I come face to face with him, blue eyes to flashing green eyes, and scream back, "How dare you criticize my life? My mother is dying, and I came to be with her. I have a responsible job in Manhattan and live with my boyfriend, who I love with all my heart."

Taken aback by my response, Marcus, at first, is speechless. His eyes change from those of a ferocious feral animal to one of sincere sorrow. We are so close I can see his bright blue eyes reflecting the aftermath of a storm trying to adjust to the soothing calmness that follows. "I am sorry about your mother. I guess it is not fair to start criticizing our lifestyles when we don't know much about each other. Maybe I should treat you like one of the bachelorettes and actually get to know you before I go forward with personal attacks."

Smiling, I reach out my hand to touch his arm. "I think that would be a good start. So, tell me Marcus, what are your expectations from being on this show?"

"I wish I knew. At first, I thought it would be fun, and I am overdue for laughs. Two and a half years of law school followed by taking the bar exam, has pretty much wiped me out. But going on these group dates is beginning to annoy me. The one-on-one dates have been helpful. I guess I am relearning how to socialize again. My dating skills are archaic and unrefined. Perhaps you can help me. Tell me what I should be doing in order to find the perfect match."

Sighing, a hundred reasons come into my thoughts about Brandon. "There is no perfect match for anyone, but if I were in your shoes, I would try to find the one person who has the same values and interests as myself. No doubt, there has to be a physical attraction, but I would seek that unique person who makes me want to be a better person. Someone who is my better half. Someone whose absence makes me sad. Someone who loves me for who I am and not what I am."

"Is that how it is for you and your boyfriend?"

"Yes."

"Then you are very fortunate to have found that special someone, Rina. I can only hope for the same. And I will take into consideration what you just said and try to take this entire dating scene seriously."

When it was time to depart and we said our goodbye, I witness a sincere sadness resonating on his face which makes me blurt out, "Good, we made some progress today, Marcus. By the way, Katie would be a good match for you."

Grinning and lightly touching his right ear, he mouths, "Thank you."

Chapter 6

Marcus, 27, Former Law Student

Startling myself, I walk away from my latest covert conversation with Rina, and I find myself wishing that she is one of the bachelorettes. She would be a perfect match for me. She is easy to talk to and intelligent, and she keeps me on my toes. She is not beautiful in a 'drop-dead gorgeous' way, but she can hold her own against any of the bachelorettes on any reality show. Plus, she can imitate an enchanting southern accent.

But Rina is not one of the bachelorettes or for that matter available. And she is out of my league. Katie, on the other hand, would be a great catch. I find her to be oddly alluring, in a captivating sporty, playful way. We joked, we laughed, and we kissed on our date. So now my goal is to convince the audience that Katie would be a faultless match for me unless the other three women with whom I have not had one-on-one dates could possibly work out.

In the meantime, I must evaluate the three remaining bachelorettes in a positive, deductive manner which brings me to tonight's plans. Arrangements have been made for a meet-and-greet speed dating spectacle. It's a very peculiar concept in which each of the bachelorettes must speed date with each bachelor in a private room. Ten minutes is the time limit in which the bachelorettes must ask fifteen up close and personal questions, and then summarize each of the bachelor's answers in a comical manner. It sounds complicated to me, and I am glad that the shoe is not on the other foot. Law briefs I can write: but writing something downright witty is not my speed.

I must admit it took some creative writing skills by the bachelorettes. Together, as a group, they summarized our answers to the following questions.

Where were you born?
Are your parents still married to each other?
What is your favorite holiday?

Do you have any siblings?
Who is your best friend?
What is your favorite sport?
Did you go to college?
Have you ever been married?
Do you have any children?
What is your favorite movie?
Who is your favorite actress/actor?
What is your favorite food?
What is your favorite color?
Do you want children?
How many?
What is your favorite vacation spot?

After asking each of us those questions on this speed date, the bachelorettes were able to summarize our answers in a very witty way.

Los Angeles Marcus can be spotted at a Laker basketball game on Christmas Day, eating mashed potatoes and drinking vodka tonics until he turns blue.

Birthday boy, Damon searches for fame as an extra on filming of Pulp Fiction in Detroit, eating macaroni and cheese with tequila shooters.

Maui Jack's mom makes yellow eggs every Christmas morning, as he watches *The Natural* with Tom Cruise.

Noah from Austin, Texas parties hard on New Year's Eve only to watch college football at a hamburger joint with his friend Tom trying to nurse a *Hangover*.

Kevin carb-loads on Thanksgiving with beer and blackened steak and potatoes, then watches football until his parents drag him back to the table to play *Clueless*.

Dr. Dusty craves green salad and pizza and manages to watch hockey on Easter day in Barcelona, Spain with his four siblings.

Each of the bachelors, including myself, enjoy the bachelorettes' play on words, and I even recognize the facetious and on-target profiling of each of us. As the night progresses into a cocktail party, it becomes evident that each bachelor gravitates toward a particular bachelorette.

For instance, Damon, the unemployed actor, seeks out the model Jessie. Noah, the oldest of the bachelors, has a knack for being a worldly conversationalist and knows a little about everything. He and Lisa seem to have hit it off on their previous one-on-one date, and every time I happen to walk by them, they are always in a heated discussion. It's a wonder that any romance can even get off the ground.

Dusty, the quietest and most reserved of all of us, in an unassuming manner, has set his sights on Greta, my next one-on-one date scheduled in two days. Including Greta, I am anxious to have a one-on-one date with the three bachelorettes left. However, these three women couldn't be more different. Greta owns her own dynamic website business in Tampa, Florida, Jessie is a runway model, and Lisa is a drop-dead gorgeous exotic dancer and unique in every way possible.

My afternoon date with Greta begins with a two-hour limousine ride to downtown San Diego which allows us plenty of time to learn about each other's lives. She fits the description of a go-getter and a woman who knows what she wants and goes after it without reservation. Her intense blue-green eyes, shadowed by thick black lashes, straight nose, and sensuous mouth create a captivating allusion of beauty and brains. She enjoys most outdoor activities, but due to a meniscus knee injury, she has retired her snowboard and has opted to return to downhill skiing.

Born and raised in Orlando, Florida, her choice to go to the University of Miami pleased her middle-class parents who are both teachers and still married to one another. She has done extensive traveling throughout the United States and hopes that her travels will include Europe one day. Surprising me just a bit, she admits she would like to get married, sooner rather than later, and have a family before she turns 30.

We have dinner at a lovely seafood restaurant on the water, and after, we stroll holding hands down the streets of San Diego, thoroughly enjoying ourselves as we explore some of the local bars. We never stop talking during the drive home, and both of us are surprised when we pull up to the houses. When we kiss goodbye, I feel an immediate attraction to Greta, and I wouldn't mind getting to know her even better.

Much to my surprise, loud, boisterous laughter welcomes me when I open the front door to the bachelor house. I find Noah, the bar owner, lying on the rug in front of the television, bare-chested, and completely manscaped with two full shot glasses on his six-pack stomach. His scrawny, but muscular legs and arms move up and down, as he tries to do sit-ups. Jack, the bodybuilder, with his tall, rugged, hard-as-a-rock body lays face down, next to Noah, performing push-ups with two filled shot glasses on his back, and as the rest of the bachelors, cheer and count. It seems to be the battle of the brutes to see who can do the most sit-ups or push-ups without spilling the shots. To no surprise to anyone, Jack wins the contest.

The next morning at breakfast, Dusty approaches me to ask how my date went with Greta, his slate gray eyes trying to read my thoughts.

"Well, Dusty, Greta seems to be a great girl. I admire her creative, ambitious nature and the fact that she is also down to earth with realistic goals of her own. We had fun on our date, and it made me realize that she is one of those girls that makes a person feel important and special. You two seem to have a special connection though. Is that why you are asking?"

Raking his fingers through his close-cropped golden-brown spiky hair, it is obvious he has something to say. "Yes, Marcus, I like Greta a lot, and I am hoping that the audience sees our special connection."

"Well, I am glad you told me how you feel and honestly, I am not sure if the "Love at First Sight" idea works for me anyway, but it sounds like you two would be good together."

"Thanks, Marcus, I hope something works out for you, too." I hope so too since now I am down to only two more bachelorettes to date. I feel a little sad about Greta, but I also know there are no guarantees when it comes to falling in love.

Chapter 7

Rina, 27, Freelance Writer

It's early Saturday morning, and I have just finished making myself a frothy cappuccino when my cell phone rings. To my utmost complete surprise, it is Brandon calling me from LAX Airport asking me to come pick him up. I am so thrown off by his call, but I am more than elated. Even though we talk nightly, I miss his naked freshly showered damp hard body sneaking into our bed at night as he pulls my bare sleeping form into his muscular arms making me feel blissful and cherished, enveloped in our cozy spoon position.

Even more arousing is the fact that I have him all to myself for the entire weekend until he returns home Sunday night. Borrowing one of Alex's extra cars and utilizing my great skills in navigating around traffic snarls, it takes me only ten minutes to drive to the airport. I immediately spot Brandon before pulling up to the baggage claim standing curbside so tall and lean, dark sunglasses hiding his sexy blue eyes. I leap out of the driver's seat and hold that handsome man in my arms so tight, both of us having a difficult time breathing normally.

Finally, I pull away and whisper into his ear, "I missed you so much. Why didn't you tell me you were coming?"

Smiling with that enigmatic charm he embraces so well, he says, "I wanted to surprise you. You have always told me I am predictable, and I wanted to prove you wrong. By the way, nice wheels."

Looking back at the sleek shiny black Maserati, I laugh, "Well, you know me with my simple tastes, I had to pick between a Porsche, Bentley, and Rolls Royce, and I settled for the mediocre one." Laughing out loud, Brandon pulls me back into his arms and plants a lust-filled kiss on my wanton lips.

On the drive home, I fill Brandon in on the latest news of my mom's health, along with updates on Susannah's progress decorating the nursery and the countdown to the birth of baby Frankie. Before we know it, we are pulling up to the enormous garage that houses up to six cars.

Even though Brandon has visited Susannah and Alex before, no one can get used to such grandeur. "Wow, it always overwhelms me to see how other people live." And we both agree that neither of us will ever live in such luxury.

Brandon has always had a special connection with my mom, and it is very transparent when her pale blue eyes light up when he walks into the kitchen.

"Oh, Brandon, you are a sight for sore eyes. What brings you to this neck of the woods?"

"Why, Rose, you should know how I can't stay away too long from your company or your daughter's." And he sweeps her thin form into his arms and gives her a gentle hug. Setting her back into a chair, he turns toward Susannah who is busy sashaying around, so he can admire her growing belly.

"Nice, Susannah, I can see you have definitely blossomed." And then he gives her a big hug, while simultaneously shaking the beaming Alex's hand.

Of course, as I witness this entire joyous greeting, I am a little disappointed. I had planned to sneak Brandon into my bedroom and remain there the entire day, hoping that no one would be any wiser that he had come to visit. But, after watching how my mom's demeanor perked up with his presence, I realize our little romantic tryst will have to wait. And, to even deflate the purring of my body, Alex announces that today would be an excellent time to invite some friends over for a barbeque. And the party begins.

Later that afternoon, after much food, drinks, and socializing, Brandon takes my hand, as the laughter and poolside music fade away and leads me across the lush expansive green lawn. The bright sun hangs high in the sky, casting its warm bright beams on a garden of colorful roses on the side of the house while reflecting a luminous glow onto the Pacific Ocean below. A quiet, hush surrounds us as we approach my most treasured spot... the secret garden and gazebo. Wearing only a sheer, gauzy cover-up over an even skimpier bikini, it doesn't take long before Brandon easily peels them away.

Within minutes, we both lay naked on the cushioned seats with Brandon's hands all over my body, his lips stifling the rapturous moans coming from my mouth. His slow, easy kisses have me moaning with delight. Beneath the swell of my breasts, his tongue flickers over my nipple, while his other hand fondles the other breast. Aching to co-join, my body and hips arch to accept him inside me. Yearning for this moment, and with a gravity of triumph, Brandon thrusts inside me. Thrashing beneath him, we are so caught up in our self-exploring moment of ecstasy until we are rudely and untimely interrupted by a noise.

I abruptly pull apart from Brandon and reach for some type of clothing to cover my bareness and scream, "Oh, my God, we can't do this here."

"Why not?"

"Brandon, you remember when I told you about the filming of that reality show next door and that I have spoken to one of the bachelors several times, well, this is where we meet. What if he sees us having sex?"

Sitting there puzzled and taken aback by my reaction, Brandon exclaims, "So what's the problem with that? I am sure he is not immune to two people in love having sex in the privacy of a backyard. It's not against the law."

"I know, but I would be embarrassed."

"Why, you have nothing to be embarrassed about. We love each other, and we enjoy each other. Making love is how humans show love. What's going on, Rina? I am not sure I understand."

Frustrated and trying to make a point, I continue, "What we do in private is sacred to me. I don't want anyone intruding on these intimate moments. It's our treasured time not to be shared with others, that's just the way I am."

Pulling me back into his arms and kissing me on the tip of my nose, he says, "I guess you are right, I just couldn't wait another minute to be inside you. It's been way too long, and I miss you. Let's go back to the privacy of your bedroom so we can finish what we started. And remember one thing, Rina. I am very selfish to what belongs to me."

I tell him that I agree with that same idea. We quickly get dressed and practically run back to the house. And the rest of the weekend took on a magical quality of sex and more sex until Sunday evening came, and it was time for Brandon to say goodbye.

***

With the weekend over and Brandon gone, this Monday morning has lost its sparkle for me as I sit in the kitchen drinking an ordinary coffee. I am not in the mood for a cappuccino or the gazebo.

When Susannah walks in, she comes up to me, puts her arms around me, and says, "I will miss him too, Rina. And, although I don't want to admit it, I think he will be back before you know it."

"Don't say that. Mom is not ready to leave us just yet. We have to believe that, don't we?"

"Yes, we do. But it just breaks my heart to see her suffer. Remember what she told us, and we must honor those wishes. She told us she does not want to be in pain, and she just wants to die peacefully. How can we make that happen?"

"Not sure, Susannah, but we will not let her be in pain, I promise."

This conversation with my sister did nothing to improve my already daunting mood. The reason I came to southern California was to spend time with my mom before she passes away, and I have to believe that I made the right choice although this long-distance relationship with Brandon really sucks.

Chapter 8

Marcus, 27, Former Law Student

Always intrigued by the voices and sounds from the other side of the block wall, with my ultimate goal to engage in another scintillating conversation with Rina, it was with utmost embarrassment that as I peeked over the wall, I witnessed two nude bodies wrapped in rapturous copulation. Immediately recognizing one of the figures, I jumped down from the bench and hightailed it out of there. Mind you, it was just a micro-second glance, but there was no mistaking that the shiny dark hair splayed out in disarray upon the cushion of the couch, her face aglow with passion, belonged to Rina.

Silently walking away, I realize that that is exactly the type of relationship that I have been longing for. Such unadulterated pleasure for each other, no inhibitions and no regrets. That type of love is a rarity, and that is exactly what I am searching for. Whether I find it with one of these six bachelorettes on this show, or somewhere else, I will not settle for less.

Tonight, I have a one-on-one date with Lisa, the exotic dancer. Knowing I must keep all of my options open, I am looking forward to learning more about this beautiful, alluring woman.

The date card, delivered by the host Neil Geiger, mentions dressing for a fabulous night of fun in downtown Los Angeles. But I am not prepared when Lisa walks out of the bachelorette house, scathed in the tiniest sequined red dress I have ever seen, her long tanned legs shimmering in the night glow. With her mass of blond hair slicked back into a bun at the nape of her neck, she looks like a goddess. Knowing that my mouth dropped open as I stood there in awe, I find it extremely difficult to speak. Smiling a smile that extends to her golden amber eyes, she takes my arm into hers, and says, "Marcus, we are going to have fun tonight." All I can do is nod my head.

The limousine drives us to a restaurant called Redbird, located in the former rectory and courtyard of the now-consecrated Cathedral of the Roman

Catholic Archdiocese of Los Angeles. We dine on exquisite seared foie gras served with tart quince, followed by succulent and juicy red wattle pork, each accompanied by a distinctive glass of wine.

I find Lisa to be an insightful and witty conversationalist, which totally surprises me. We discuss stock market choices and her view on politics, and she gives me an astute analysis of all the bachelors and bachelorettes on the show. She confides to me that she has a master's degree in Psychology from Stanford and to pay for her education, she began to dance for money. She loves dancing and will continue to be an exotic dancer until her looks or her body gives out.

After dinner, the limousine driver maneuvers his car into a dank, dark alley which makes me skeptical at first, especially when I notice an extremely long line of people standing along the side of one of the buildings. Escorted by the driver to the front of the line, we enter through a dented galvanized metal door, to be immediately surrounded by pulsing music and flashing lights.

The look on Lisa's face is mesmerizing. It's obvious she feels at home, but I for one, need another drink. We are seated in the back corner at a table for two, totally stocked with bottles of vodka, rum, whiskey, and champagne. Now, I feel at home as I have our waitress quickly whip up a dirty martini for me and a glass of champagne for Lisa.

Seated side by side, I can tell that Lisa is anxious to dance by the sly looks she keeps casting my way. But all I can think about is the fact that she dances for a living, and even though I don't necessarily have two left feet, I am not sure I can measure up to her standards. I need courage to make this move so I down my martini and signal for another.

Just about this time, a gentleman dressed like a model in a GQ magazine comes up to our table and asks Lisa to dance. Now I am not sure if this is allowed on a one-on-one date, but I don't see any harm in the matter, so I tell Lisa to go right ahead and that I will watch. She never takes her eyes off mine as she begins to move around the floor in a very sexy manner. The man she is dancing with cannot take his eyes off her body, as she gyrates in a very erotic way. He tries to pull her close with his lecherous hands, but she would not allow him to touch her and easily manipulates herself far from his reach.

I am very turned on, and I can tell she is enjoying the look of lust in my eyes as well. Suddenly, much to my surprise, I recognize another figure on the dance floor. Unbelievably, Rina is at the same nightclub, and she is dancing with the nerdiest man I have ever seen. As she dances closer to where I am sitting, she looks in my direction, stumbles, and trips right into my lap.

"Marcus," she screams, "what are you doing here?"

"Well, Rina, I guess I should ask the same of you. I am out on a date, and you just fell into my lap. I can't wait to introduce you to her." Her look of total surprise is priceless.

"I am so sorry. When I saw you sitting there, I lost my balance. Where is your date, by the way?"

I point toward the dance floor and say, "She is warming up. I am such a fantastic dancer she feels the need to practice first."

Her nose wrinkles up, and she states, "Oh, that's a little odd, but I guess I understand." And then she remembers her dancing partner and smiles, "I would like to introduce you to my brother-in-law, Alex. Alex, this is Marcus. He is one of the bachelors from the reality show being taped in your neighborhood."

"Hi, Marcus, nice to meet you. I haven't been watching the show, but I heard my wife and Rina discuss the dynamics of the program, and it sounds very exciting indeed."

Startled by this gathering, Lisa walks up and is somewhat perplexed. "Marcus, are these some friends of yours?"

"Yes, I guess you can say that, but our meeting was not planned. Lisa, I would like to introduce you to Rina and Alex. Let's just say that they are neighbors with whom I have run into now and then."

"Well, that's nice," Lisa says. "So are you ready to show me some of your moves, Marcus? I think it's about time." Lisa reaches for my hand and leads me out onto the dance floor.

And I show her some moves. Although everyone's eyes are on Lisa as she dominates the dance floor. At least I feel I am able to make a lesser fool of myself. Every once in a while, I find myself searching for a glimpse of Rina, but she seems to have left for the night.

By the end of the evening, it is obvious to both Lisa and I that we enjoy each other's company and there is no denying the physical attraction between us. When we kiss the sparks definitely do fly. Can I see us together forever? That is difficult to say, but we do make a very exciting couple.

***

Waking up in the early morning, with the weather cool and overcast, it comes to me that I am way overdue for an intense jog around the neighborhood. After donning my sweats and jogging shoes and silently exiting out the front door, I inhale the damp and salty morning air. I have always enjoyed this time of the morning when no other soul is around, no cars to obstruct the clean air, just me enjoying the moment.

Caught up with lust-filled thoughts about my date with Lisa last night, I notice a single person ahead of me heading for the jogging trail along the beach. As this person makes a move to hug the curve up ahead, I watch as the jogger's foot catches a fallen tree branch and falls to the ground.

Not close enough, to offer my hand, I am surprised when the figure does not immediately stand back up but continues to lay on the pathway face down. Once I reach the fallen body, I can tell that she is female and unconscious. Turning the body over to evaluate her condition and check her pulse, I realize that it is Rina.

Noticing a cut on her head, I reach for her neck praying for a pulse, which there is. I yell, "Rina, wake up, please. Tell me what hurts." Not knowing what else to do, I take my water bottle and empty it onto her bleeding head, hoping to wake her up, which I do.

She screams instantly reaching for her head, "Why did you do that? And why are you here?"

"I saw you fall and when I reached you, you wouldn't wake up, and I got worried. What was I supposed to do?"

"I don't know, but did the water have to be freezing?"

"I am sorry, Rina. I am so glad you are okay. Besides your head, is there anything else that hurts?"

"Yes, my ankle hurts. I am not sure I can walk. But, mostly my pride. I can't believe that you got to witness this mishap."

"Well, it is not the first time I saw you trip. Do you remember last night?"

"Of course, I do, I didn't hit my head that hard."

"Don't be touchy. Let me help you up, and we can see how bad your ankle hurts."

I lift her up, and she feels so light. "Can you put any weight on your left ankle?"

"No, I don't think so. It hurts too much."

Looking back toward the houses on the bluff, I realize that we are a good mile from home. Forgoing my desire to keep running, I say, "Lean your left side on me, and let's see if we can make it on our own. If not, we will call for someone to pick you up. You did bring your cell phone."

"No."

"Rina, you should never go jogging alone, especially this early in the morning without your cell phone. It's dangerous. What would you have done if I wasn't here?" I ask.

"I know, I know. It's just that I wasn't thinking clearly when I left the house. I woke up early because I had a crazy dream about YOU! Oh darn, I didn't want to admit that. See what you made me do."

"Whoa, don't be getting on my case. I am sorry you had a sex dream about me."

"I did not have a sex dream about you!"

"Are you sure?"

"What do you think of me, Marcus? I am living with another man. Of course, it wasn't a sex dream. It was just a weird dream about clouds and dancing. I guess because I saw you dancing last night, and you may have been on my mind. By the way, how did your date go? I can't believe you let her dance with someone else on your date. Is that allowed?"

"I don't know. Maybe they will cut that part out of the scene, and I hope that they don't cut out the part when you sat on my lap." Chuckling.

"I did not sit on your lap. I tripped."

"Well, Ms. Spencer, you seem to have a habit of tripping, don't you?"

"Ha, ha, you are such a funny man. Stop talking and help me walk home before Christmas gets here."

Rina is able to put a little weight on her left ankle, so actually the trek home went by quickly. We talk about last night, and I tell her that Lisa has surprised me with her college background and her ability to come across as a very intelligent woman. Rina confides in me that she thinks Lisa is the most beautiful woman she has ever seen. I will have to agree with that analysis.

I ring the doorbell, only to be greeted with hysteria by a short and stout woman.

She screams, "Oh my, Ms. Rina, what has happened? You look as white as a ghost. What happened to your head?" And then she yells even louder, "Ms. Susannah, come quickly. Rina has been hurt."

Two women come to the front door, the elder being pushed in a wheelchair. There is no doubt recognizing the mother-daughter relationship between the two. They look so much alike.

Finally, Rina chimes in, "Marcus, you remember meeting my mother, Rose, and this is my sister, Susannah." And then she continues, "I had a fall, and Marcus was so kind enough to help me home. I think I twisted my ankle, but I am okay other than that."

"But your head," her mother says. "You have blood dripping down the side of your face. We need to clean that right away before an infection sets in. Susannah, get me some rubbing alcohol, a bowl of warm water, a bucket of ice, and some clean gauze."

Laughing and turning toward Marcus, Rina states, "My mom is a nurse. She knows what needs to be done. Thank you so much, Marcus, for helping me home."

Not ready to leave just yet, I say, "Rose, direct me to where you want Rina to sit." Rose proceeds to bark orders to Susannah insisting she be wheeled to the kitchen, so I easily pick up Rina into my arms, who is protesting the entire time, and carry her into the kitchen, setting her down onto a kitchen chair. Recognizing that everything is under control after hearing many 'thank yous' from each of them, I take my leave.

Chapter 9

Rina Spencer, 27, Freelance Writer

Today is one of those days I wish I could erase. But, actually, if I am honest about everything, I have to admit that this disaster of a day began last night.

It all started when I saw Marcus sitting at this trendy nightclub, and I tripped and fell onto his lap. Not that nightclubs are my scene, but Alex had asked me to come along for kicks when he and Susannah were invited by his company to attend a dinner and dance outing. I agreed after much pleading by Susannah. Alex loves to dance, but his dance style is not something I would brag about. When I was out on the dance floor with Alex, I spotted Marcus; I lost my footing.

I was more than embarrassed by being caught dancing with my stumbling, two-left-footed brother-in-law Alex, then by my falling. I handled my emotions very well during my confrontation with Marcus, but I just wanted to get out of that place as fast as I could. But, when I saw Marcus stand up to dance a slow song with Lisa, I couldn't stop myself from watching them. They seemed to mold into each other as if they were one body, and he kept whispering into her ear, and she would look at him with her sultry eyes and pouty red lips and smile coquettishly. They truly seemed to be enjoying themselves, and I could feel a strong chemistry connection between them, and I felt a pang of jealousy. Not for Marcus, but I wanted to be in the arms of my boyfriend and enjoy those romantic moments, too.

And then later that night, I had a crazy dream about Marcus. I was dancing in his arms, and he was looking down at me as if I was the only girl in the world. I was smiling up and when he lowered his lips to mine, we kissed. I immediately woke myself up from the dream, but it continued to haunt me all night long.

When morning finally came, I needed to do something out of the ordinary and decided to go for a run. Jogging is not really my thing. I was so concentrating on my breathing, trying to forget about last night when I lost my footing and fell. To my shock and disappointment, I was rudely cold-splashed awakened by the one person to witness my complete humiliation... Marcus. And he is whom I was trying to forget.

How does a girl get into these predicaments? Of course, Marcus, the gentleman and kind soul that he is, carries me back to Susannah's house and puts me in the trusting hands of my dear mother. When he left, I was speechless, which is a rarity for me. Humiliation has a sobering effect on many people, especially me. I know for sure that I never want to face him again.

But of course, fate doesn't listen to those demands. As I am hobbling around the kitchen the next morning trying to make a cappuccino, the doorbell rings. And who should come walking through the kitchen escorted by the maid Mary, is Marcus himself, carrying a huge bouquet of daisies.

Smiling, exposing those damn sexy dimples, he says, "I would like to present these to the woman who just cannot stop herself from falling head over heels for me."

Initially, I want to snap at him and respond with a smart remark, but he looks so sweet standing there, all I can say is, "Thank you, Marcus."

"So how is the ankle doing?" Noting the container of frothed milk in my hand, he continues, "I could sure use a good cappuccino myself. The boys at the house enjoy strong, black coffee only, no foo-foo stuff for those macho men."

"Sure, I can whip you up one, too, since I just started making mine. My ankle is a little sore, but it's not stopping me from getting around." Sensing an awkward silence, I plunge right in, "So tell me, Marcus, what are your thoughts on Lisa? You two seem to get along rather well, especially on the dance floor."

Rubbing the back of his neck, as if trying to figure out what I just asked, he responds with, "Yeah, she is a very special girl, and I was definitely attracted to her. But I am not sure she is the right one for me. I want someone who is my equal, in every way. She is smart enough, sweet enough, and all that, but I don't think that I like it when other men cannot keep their eyes off of her when she dances. She is incredible on the dance floor, and I am not sure I can handle the attention she gets."

Something inside me wants to yell hallelujah, but instead, I tell him that I understand because I feel the same way. Not sure what has come over me, I do not back away when Marcus walks over to me, looks directly into my eyes, reaches out, and touches my hair.

"Your hair reminds me of black velvet," and then touching my cheek, he mutters, "And your skin feels like satin." His muscle-tensed arms wrap around my waist, pulling me in closer while his thighs press hard against mine. We remain close for a long throbbing moment before I come to my senses and push him away from me.

Laughing to cover up my embarrassment and the fact that being that close to him caused me to lean in closer, "Why don't you save those lines and moves for one of your bachelorettes? I am sure they are wondering where you have gone off to." I feel a little breathless with the effort of speaking.

After meticulously taking the last sip of his cappuccino, a slow grin crosses Marcus' face, watching my facial reaction very closely. Then glancing outside, "You are right, I better get going. I told them I was going out for a run, so I need to build up a little sweat before heading back to the house."

Jolted from my confused thoughts and remembering my manners, I mutter, "Thanks for the flowers, Marcus. They are one of my favorites."

"Happy to oblige, Rina." Revealing a devilish grin, "I hope your sister doesn't mind, but I stole these flowers from the side of the house. There were so many of them. I couldn't stop myself. Take care of your foot so that we can meet again in our secret garden."

After that comment, I am smiling when he leaves. But then I remind myself to stop it. It is dangerous for me to be around him alone. Vaguely annoyed for allowing him such an intimate liberty, it's best to pretend this never happened. Even though he makes me laugh, and I am always happy to see him, I need to remind myself that he is not my bachelor.

Chapter 10

Marcus, 27, Former Law Student

Why do producers of the show try to change things? I understand that the sole purpose of a reality show or any show is to increase ratings. But, this time, they have gone too far and decided to throw a wrench at us that no one is expecting. A talent show... a "Love at First Sight" first. Next week all the bachelors and bachelorettes will be expected to compete in a talent show, and we get to invite our parents. Really? Why in the world would I want my parents to be involved in this fiasco in the first place?

And, secondly, there is no way my parents will agree to come. Not only do parents get to witness our so-called talent, but they also will get the opportunity to give their opinions on who to match up with whom. My parents think the show is ludicrous as it is and now the show expects them to be involved in the matching. NO WAY!!! Can't imagine what they will say when they get the text inviting them on the show.

Seeking out the only person I wish to share my thoughts with, I peek over the block wall. I am disappointed when I don't see Rina sitting at her favorite spot in the gazebo. I guess this revelation about the talent show will have to wait. Going back to the house, I can't stop thinking about the talent show. Lucky for me, my parents forced me to learn how to pick a guitar at the ripe age of six.

Along with that talent, I can croon a country song like Garth Brooks. Hah, just kidding, but at least I can keep a tune. I also can't keep myself from thinking about the bachelors in the house and what they will choose as their particular talent. The macho men will probably choose beer chugging or an exposition on weightlifting.

I also am intrigued to see what the bachelorette's hidden talents are. This will definitely be an interesting night.

The big day is here, and it is obvious that all of us are nervous about performing on national television, let alone in front of our parents. Peeking out at the audience, I am not surprised that I do not see the smiling faces of my parents, even though I hoped they would change their minds. After sending the invitation to attend the talent show, I received an immediate response from my mother that she was sorry they already had dinner plans with some friends that night and will not be able to attend. Typical, and accepted on my part.

As the evening approached, it was obvious all of us were nervous. There was a random selection for the order of the performances, and thankfully I am one of the last.

Lisa, 25, exotic dancer, is lucky enough to be number 1 and I can't help but admire the bulging muscles of her thighs underneath her sheer flowing ballet skirt, as she proceeds to entertain us on pointe ballet to the song *Just the Way You Are* by Bruno Mars. As she glides across the floor, we all watch her with awe.

Next is Jack, 27, real estate broker. He surprises us all when a player piano is rolled out to the stage, and he entertains us with a mock concert by the pianist Liberace. Wearing a glittery jacket and huge bobbled, diamond rings on every finger, Jack shows us why Liberace was known as 'Mr. Showman'.

Katie, 24, fashion sales, regales us with a musical rendition of *Somewhere Over the Rainbow*. Wearing a simple long black evening gown, her hair in a ponytail at the top of her head falls down in ringlets. Her voice is strong and surreal, totally in control of the song, and magical in every way.

Cheyenne, 24, college student, makes the perfect choice. She plays a song on the flute which brings tears to my eyes, it is so enchanting and soulful. If I were a cobra, I would have been tamed for sure.

Damon, 27, self-employed, initially had a hard time deciding which talent to use. Actually, he confided in me that he is probably the least talented person I will ever know. We came up with an idea that works for him and should interest everyone in the process. He used his selling techniques to create a video presentation, 'How to invest your millions'. Public speaking is definitely his forte, and I am ready to follow his lead as soon as I make my first million.

Kevin, 29, gym owner/bodybuilder, is no surprise to any of us. Outfitted in tight-fitting workout clothes that accentuates his bulging muscles, brings out a yoga mat, and begins to position his body in yoga poses that I have never imagined our bodies were capable of.

Greta, 24, entrepreneur, looking as cute as can be, dressed in black leather and lace, surprises us all, by belting out a rap song that sounds like she can rival Jay-Z. Nothing is more exciting to me than to see a female compete with the big guns. Way to go, Greta!

Noah, 29, bar owner, using the only talent that he has, entertains us with a full bottle of tequila on his forehead as he proceeds to pour ten shots of liquor into shot glasses without looking and/or spilling an ounce or dropping the bottle from his forehead. It is impressive to watch.

Jesse, 25, model, talent choice is spot on. She pretends to be in a fashion show and does a high fashion catwalk in a very tiny spandex red bikini with matching stiletto heels that is so seductive and sexy, it embarrassingly turns me on.

Trying to cover up my embarrassing excitement, I am thankful I have my guitar as a cover. I walk out onto the stage crooning Garth Brook's most popular song *Friends in Low Places* while I pick the guitar. It was the audience's choice to sing along with me, and I feel that I did an awesome rendition of the song.

Amanda, 27, unemployed, as clever as can be, decides to reenact a scene from *Gone with the Wind* mimicking Vivian Leigh's Scarlet O'Hara and her most defiant speech vowing to survive following the aftermath of the Civil War. Dressed in an old raggedy, dirty dress, streaks of brown dirt smeared on her face, her dyed brown hair spilling out in several places from the loose bun pulled back at the nape of her neck, she is the spitting image of Scarlett. Looking out at the audience with a proud, smug look on her face, she recites, *"As God is my witness, they're not going to lick me. I'm going to live through this, and when it's all over, I'll never be hungry again—nor any of my folks. If I have to lie, steal, cheat, or kill, as God is my witness, I'll never be hungry again."*

A very moving and believable monologue and her southern accent can only be matched by two people I know, Vivian Leigh and Rina Spencer. I am definitely a sucker for Southern accents. Maybe she should try acting since currently she is unemployed and searching for her next job.

Dusty, 25, medical intern, as our final act, shows up in a dapper tuxedo and recites the poem by Elizabeth Barrett Browning, *How Do I Love Thee?* His eyes sought out Greta during his act, and it was obvious to all of us how smitten he is with her. His voice, so deep and strong, very appropriate and perfect to summarize our entire journey on this show.

At the end of all of the performances, the cheering and clapping from the parents, as well as us, makes us all very proud.

Not caring who wins the talent show, I choose to leave the parents and the others to mingle, reaching out to the one person I want to talk to tonight. Instead of peeking over the block wall, I decide to tell the show staff that I need to go for a walk. Of course, as you can imagine, my steps lead me to the massive door of Rina's sister's home. Hesitantly knocking, I am surprised when Rina answers the door, instead of the maid Mary.

"Hi, Marcus. I am just watching the show. What are you doing out here when you should be with all the other bachelors and bachelorettes? The show isn't over."

"I know. My parents decided that they didn't want to be a part of me making a fool of myself."

"Wait, you didn't make a fool of yourself. I really enjoyed your guitar playing, and you also have a very decent voice, surprisingly." Raising her eyebrows in approval.

"Decent voice? Surprisingly, am I supposed to take that as a compliment, Rina?" chuckling. "Would you mind going for a walk around the block with me, I can use the company."

"Sure, let me grab a sweater and let Susannah know where I am going."

While we silently walk, I can see Rina occasionally glancing at me.

Breaking the silence, Rina speaks first. "OK, Marcus. What is going on? I don't think I have ever spent five minutes with you without you speaking. Something is going on. Am I right?"

Intuitive as usual, I am glad that she recognizes my sour mood. "Yes, Rina, there is something wrong. It's my parents. I don't like to complain, and usually, it doesn't bother me, but my parents are the coldest people I know. No matter what I do, it is always the wrong choice. They hate the fact that I am on this show, and not showing up tonight is a slap again in my face."

"Everyone knows who my parents are, and their choice to not show up will not be missed or misconstrued. They have never been proud of anything I have accomplished, and I wish I didn't want their approval so much, but I do. I worked hard to get where I am, and they never gave me any credit. What is wrong with them, or better yet, what is wrong with me?"

Grabbing my arm and turning me toward her, she takes my hands and looks straight into my eyes with her twinkling green eyes. "Nothing is wrong with you, but everything is wrong with them. If you were my son, I would be so proud of you and want to show you every day."

Standing here in the middle of a sidewalk, looking into each other's eyes, I can't stop myself. I put my arms around her waist and pull her in close, bending down, my lips search out the softness of hers, and in that moment, I lose myself. It isn't for more than a few seconds before she abruptly pulls away from me. But, in those few seconds, I feel a longing desire for this beautiful woman. It is unlike anything I have ever felt before, but I also do not want to lose her.

"Rina, I am so sorry. That should not have happened. That was not my intention at all tonight, but what you just said to me about being proud of me if you were my mother, I was so touched. Let's just pretend this kiss did not happen, OK?"

Flustered and confused, I can tell that Rina is trying to pull herself together. "OK, Marcus, I know you have been feeling sorry for yourself, and I will forgive you, but only this one time. Don't you ever take advantage of a situation like you just did? Do you promise me?"

"Of course," I answer weakly. But, later that night, I can't stop thinking about that kiss and how it made me feel. There is something between us, no denying that fact.

Chapter 11

Rina Spencer, 27, Freelance Writer

I went to bed that night remembering the brief contact of Marcus' lips on mine and had a very difficult time falling asleep.

The next morning, I wake up excited but exhausted. Later this afternoon, my brothers Scott and Randall will be arriving, and I am so looking forward to spending time with them. However, my only fear is that they are coming for the wrong reason, and I am hoping that once they notice and witness the deterioration of our mother, they will change their minds about the true reason for their visit.

My mother Rose is in extra good spirits, and she seems to have more energy than usual. She had me dress her in one of her favorite outfits; Saint John black slacks, a cream-colored cashmere sweater, and her flat black Tory Burch shoes. My mom has always enjoyed wearing designer clothes, and today is no exception.

When the boys walk through the front door, the loud ruckus they make is reminiscent of every time they walk into our house back in Long Island. I can see the excitement in my mother's eyes, so I push her wheelchair from the kitchen to meet the boys halfway. When she catches sight of them, she yells out in a high-pitched shriek, I never knew she was capable of.

"Is that my Frank coming to visit?" This startles us all.

"No, Mom," Susannah says, "It is your boys, Randall and Scott."

Scowling at Susannah, my mom laughs, "Of course it is. Do you think I don't recognize my own children?"

We all were not sure what just happened, but for a split second, the look in my brothers' eyes said it all. It was as if they didn't recognize their own mother. But I couldn't help but wonder if my mom didn't recognize them. Whatever the case, I am so glad that my mom is so preoccupied with trying to reach for them, she doesn't notice their blank looks. But Susannah, Alex, and I have seen it, and it is heartbreaking to witness.

After picking my mom out of the chair, squeezing her in a big bear hug, and then passing her onto Scott, Randall speaks first, of course, "We brought you a surprise, Mom." Behind the boys, out steps two people. One I recognize as Scott's life partner, Chuck, but the woman I did not.

"Mom, I would like you to meet my new wife, Granada" beams Randall. Now this is earth-shattering news to all of us, especially since my mom has asked us numerous times to never marry without her being a witness. I expected a bomb to drop. But, much to my surprise, my mom responds out of character. She sits back down on the chair and looks from Randall and Granada, giving us all a huge smile, "Well, it's about time. Welcome to this crazy Spencer family, Granada." And we all laugh to stifle the tension.

Afterward, Randall happily fills us in on how he and Granada met and why he proposed marriage only one week after their initial meeting. They met on the European cruise that my brothers recently took. Granada's family is originally from Croatia but now lives in upstate New York. As a college graduation gift for their only child, Granada's parents decided that the family should take a European cruise that includes Croatia. It so happens that on the first night on the cruise, my brothers and Chuck were seated at the same dining table as Granada and her parents.

Scott pipes in, "There was an instant attraction for both Randall and Granada; it was obvious to everyone around". Chuck nods his head in agreement.

Gazing at Granada, it strikes me that she could be my sister. She is petite with shiny pale blonde hair styled in a long bob and looks just like a younger version of my mother and sister Susannah. I notice how my brother cannot keep his hands from caressing Granada's arm every time he mentions her name and how she looks up at him with two twinkling cornflower-blue eyes. Like I said before, my brother Randall is a big cuddly teddy bear, and he has finally found his soulmate.

"The reason we got married so quickly is because I came up with this brilliant idea to get married on the ship while we were docked in Croatia. It took a lot of time planning all the necessary arrangements, and of course, Granada's parents were just as stunned as you all are and wary of the entire process. But my smooth coaxing convinced them that I truly love their daughter. Randall was my best man, Chuck was a groomsman and Granada's mom, Liz, was her matron of honor. I guess you can say that we rushed into matrimony, but I don't think time would have made any difference because we couldn't be happier." And Randall turns to kiss Granada full on the lips. "Mom, just like you, it was "Love at First Sight" for both of us."

Most of us are still shell-shocked about the news, so Alex decides to break the ice.

"Then it is time to celebrate. Let's open some champagne and toast the new bride and groom."

After numerous toasts, laughter, and late-night snacking, Randall and Granada continue to share with us their adventures on the cruise, while Chuck and Scott give us the comical narration. Mom drifted off to sleep many times, which finally reminded us all that it was time to call it a night.

The next afternoon, we decide to play the game Monopoly. This game became one of our favorite board games when we were living in Long Island, once the twins were old enough to understand the game. This game can go on for hours, and we can see that Rose is getting a little tired, so we decide to call it quits. When we all begin to put the game away and bring the dirty dishes to the kitchen, our dear mother decides to drop a bomb on us.

"It is time you should all know that your father did not die on September 11."

We are speechless.

"Mom," Susannah finally cries out, "Dad died that day. Why are you saying this?"

"Now, Susannah, don't cry. I am sorry I never told you sooner."

We all sit back down with stunned looks upon our faces, thinking this can't be true.

"I had hoped to keep this secret to myself, but something inside me has been eating away a portion of my heart; it could be cancer, but I also think it is the guilt of not telling you the truth."

It is my turn to ask, "Mom, do you have any proof that this is true, such as letters, photos, or something like that?"

"No, just my memory."

I hear a sigh of relief go around the table as we all roll our eyes.

Continuing, I ask, "OK, Mom, then why did you accept the survivor's relief compensation offered to families of first responders who died?"

"Well, that is easy. They offered it to me, and I had no proof that he didn't die that day. What was I supposed to do? I had a family to take care of."

"Have you heard from Dad since that day, Mom?" I ask.

"Yes."

None of us know what to say. We are grieving again for our father, our mother, and the truth.

The next morning, I can't wait to get my brothers aside so that we can have a serious conversation about Mom. I am not surprised when Randall and Scott step into the kitchen and Randall says, "We need to talk. What the hell is going on with Mom? I know she has lung cancer, but have you forgotten to feed her? She looks like one of those bony, scary skeletons hanging in a doctor's office. And what about her mind, is she losing that, too?"

Holding up my hands to ward off their attack, I say, "You have no idea what is going on. While you two were gallivanting around Europe, Susannah and I have been taking care of your mother. She is too thin because she doesn't have an appetite, not because we are not feeding her. Her memory has been superb so far, but last night was a first for us, too. Tell me, my dear brothers, what did you expect when you visited?"

"That's right you two," Susannah comes rushing into the kitchen. "What did you expect?"

Tongue-tied for once, Randall just stands there, but Scott speaks up, "Wait a second, don't be jumping on us for something we didn't do. We have no idea what lung cancer does to a person. We got here as soon as we could. It's not our fault that the cancer was so advanced. We didn't expect to see anything but our Mom. But that shell of a person is not our Mom."

Susannah speaks up instantly, "Don't you dare talk about my mom that way. You two are so self-absorbed in your own lives. I am surprised you can fit us into your busy schedules before she dies. Did you not notice that your mother was so excited to see you last night? That's right, she doesn't look well, but let me tell you, she remembers everything about you two. She has been reminiscing for days."

Randall finally finds his voice, "But she didn't remember us, Sis, she called us Frank."

"If I count how many times I called you Frank, Rina, or Mom when you two were young punks before I remembered your names, I would be a rich woman."

Smiling and trying to use his charms, Randall says, "But Susannah you are a rich woman."

"Ha ha," she responds.

Susannah is in control, and she starts out by saying, "First rule of thumb, I do not want to hear any negative or mean words about our mother. She is in good hands with hospice, and she will never suffer. Secondly, our purpose, as her children, is to spend as much quality time with her as possible. Do not bring up the fact that her cancer is due to her exposure at Ground Zero; of course, it is. But it was her choice to be there. We are not going to ask for more compensation, we are not going to talk to any lawyers, we are going to let it go. Can you do this, Randall and Scott? Can you let your mother die peacefully?"

Randall speaks up first, "I don't know if I can. If the government is willing to compensate us for our mother dying too early with cancer caused by the fumes and gasses at Ground Zero, why wouldn't we ask?"

"Because I won't allow it," Susannah butts in. "When Mom dies, you will inherit plenty. Let's leave it alone and enjoy this time with Mom."

Scott, always the practical one, says, "I get it, Susannah. I was ready to go to battle for Mom, but it won't change the fact that she is dying." Touching Randall's shoulder, he continues, "I just want to be here for Mom. I don't want to fight over trivial things, let's just let it go, okay?"

Knowing how hard this is for Randall, I want to go over and put my arms around him and tell him everything is going to be okay, but I don't have to. He is maturing right before my eyes as he stands up and motions to us all to gather into a group hug.

***

We all agree that we need to come up with a plan, so I suggest one. "Let's keep our voices down before we wake up the entire neighborhood. I think it is time for the four of us to have a very serious discussion without accusations, okay?"

We head outside toward the gazebo, full, steamy coffee cups in hand. And this is our plan. First of all, it is evident we must talk to our Mom and get further details. Thankfully, although our mother's mind may not be as sharp as it used to be, we believe that she should be able to answer some questions. Most importantly, why did she wait so long to divulge this information?

Anxious to have another discussion with our Mom, we agree to gather in the kitchen later in the day, once our mother is awake and alert.

***

Her voice is a monotone; she tells us, "He intentionally disappeared on September 11. He saw the opportunity, and he took it. This is a long story, and I will start at the beginning. Your father during a routine stop at a local convenience store to pick up donuts for his station on the morning of August 30, 2001, witnessed the brutal murder of a store owner and his wife by a crime lord of the Connici family. Your father barely escaped himself. Although it was too late to save the couple, he called 911 and reported the crime."

"One week later, federal authorities contacted your father and told him that he was the sole eyewitness to a major crime involving the mafia, and they insisted that he testify. They promised that they would do their best to keep your father's identity out of the paper, but since there was no guarantee that his name would not be leaked during the trial, they insisted that our entire family enter the witness protection program. Your father was deeply torn with this request."

"Loyalty and integrity weighed heavily on his mind. Our entire lives were about to change, drastically for the worse. After hours of discussions between your father and me, the wheels were set in motion for all of us to mysteriously disappear. Your father was scheduled to testify on September 14, 2001."

"But, when September 11, 2001 occurred, your father saw an opportunity to change the course of these events. In order to protect us, he actually faked his death that day and contacted the US Marshals and told them that he found a way out of the whole mess. He would agree to testify, and he would enter the Witness Protection himself, but only if they would do two things for him. And that was to make sure that his family was not only protected but taken care of financially."

"Now please understand that I wasn't aware of these details. I did believe that your father died that terrible day and did not find out the truth until two months later. Should I have told all of you then, maybe, but it wouldn't have changed anything. Your father was never coming back. We all needed to grieve."

"He sacrificed his entire life in order to keep us protected. There was always a chance that the Connici family would come after us if your father's name was ever leaked, but the federal authorities did everything they could to keep that information sealed, and to this very day, I believe that there is no record of the true identity of the eyewitness who testified against the Connici family that day."

"Why am I telling you this now? I can see the shock and betrayal on all of your faces. So much time has gone by, and the guilt is tearing me up inside. I never married because your father and I have been meeting secretly for the past 18 years. It has always surprised me that none of you have ever wondered why I never remarried. Of course, I have always said that there was only one man in my life that I will ever love, and that fact still remains true."

Susannah, her face lined with trailing tears, said, "How could you do that to us? Don't you think we had the right to know that he is alive and safe? And what annoys me most is that you took that survivors relief money, knowing that Dad did not die that day."

"Now wait a minute. You don't know the entire story. I did not want that money from the beginning. It was not my choice. But, after much insistence by the federal authorities, I knew I had no choice. It was part of the deal. It was important to make it look like your father died that day, for our safety. Your father, in my eyes, was a hero for what he sacrificed. I only agreed to the terms because I had no way to support you and that money allowed me to go to nursing school and make something of myself."

"So where is Dad right now? Where does he live? How come he isn't here? This makes no sense to me, and besides, how do we know that you are of sane mind? I don't believe it is the truth. I think you are making this all up, and I cannot even begin to understand why." Susannah continues to look at our mother with contempt.

"Please understand that I am telling the truth, and in order to keep us safe, along with your father, the whereabouts of your father have never been revealed to me. I am unable to contact your father directly. We have a private system of sending coded messages in the want ads. He told me that every September 11, I was to search the want ads in the *New York Times* for a message from 'Sacrificed4u.'"

"Usually, the message included a coded location and date for me to meet him. He would choose remote places, such as the Poconos Mountains, the Ozarks, and Oshkosh, Minnesota. Places that were off the beaten track, just in case someone was looking for him. Whenever I told you that I was going on my annual two-week church retreat, it was to be with your father. Your father only did what he did to keep you safe. You have to forgive him and me for making these choices."

"Great," I say. "How can the mafia still be after Dad after all this time?"

"Your father never wanted to take that chance. He became a very private and paranoid person once he left, always looking over his shoulders. Always a proud man, your father had to start a new life. He could no longer be a fireman. He needed to just blend in with the masses, and he became a traveling salesman for fire and hazard control equipment."

"Now I get it," I say. "The reason you are telling us now is because September is approaching. You want us to contact Dad, don't you?"

"Yes. I usually respond to his message with the simple word 'Always4u' to let him know that I will meet him. That's what I need you to do for me. But, instead of just 'always4u' I want you to put 'Notalways4u'. He knows what that means."

"And what does that mean, Mom?" Randall asks, totally perturbed.

"He will know that I will be unable to meet him. We came up with this plan, just in case. If I don't answer the ad, he will never know the truth about whether or not I am dead or alive, but if I answer with 'Notalways4u', he will know that I am saying goodbye. He will understand what it means."

"This is crazy. Can you hear what you are saying? Why don't we respond with Susannah's address? Don't you think we deserve to see our father, too?"

"He won't come. I know he won't."

Watching our mother pour out her soul is heartbreaking. We have no idea what the truth is, but we all agree that we need to investigate further.

After putting our mother to bed later that evening, we are all stunned and overwhelmed by the news that our father is still alive although we still don't know if Rose is telling us the truth. None of us ever expected this turn of events; and if it is all true, we all need time to absorb this shocking news.

But to provide a distraction, Susannah and I decide to lighten the mood. And we tell Scott, Chuck, Randall, and Granada about the filming of the reality show next door. Intrigued, they insist on watching the finale of the show tonight with us. With all of us huddled together in the entertainment room, we anxiously wait for the audience's choice. When the host, Neil Geiger, announces the live vote results, my disappointment is obvious when I yell out 'noooo' a little too loud. And Randall calls me out on it.

"Come on, Rina. Don't tell me you take this farce of a show seriously?"

"No, I don't take this show seriously, but I have a vested interest in this show. As a friend of the bachelor Marcus, I am hoping to get the real scoop on the show from him and write an article about it."

Susannah jumps in, "Rina has been having secret rendezvous meetings with Marcus. He has been her savior more than once. She literally fell on his lap at a nightclub, and he carried her home one morning after she tripped while out jogging. I think she is jealous of Lisa and Marcus."

Before I could object, Randall asks, "What would Brandon think about this, Rina?"

"Stop it right now and leave Brandon out of this." My anger showing, I continue. "My contact with Marcus is for one reason only, I believe the success of the show is based on false ratings, and I want to be the one to uncover the farce. After all, I do write for an entertainment magazine. I am just a little upset about the result because I think Katie would have been a better match for Marcus, that's all." The rolling of their eyes makes me realize they don't believe me.

The following morning, still angry at my siblings, I am hiding in my usual spot, and am surprised to hear, "Hey, it's been a while. How's the ankle doing?"

Smiling and happy for the distraction, I say, "Doing just fine, Marcus. And how are you these days? Are you happy with who the audience picked for you? Lisa seems like a really awesome girl."

"Yes, I am. Remember, I told you that I don't believe in love at first sight. I am willing to take my chances. And, besides, we only need to date for three months, and then we both will receive some monetary compensation, so no worries for either of us if it doesn't work out."

Jumping in quickly, I ask, "Wait, are you telling me that the producers will pay you to stay together for three months? I knew it, I thought the show was a farce to begin with. Their success rate seems too high to be real."

"Wait, that's not what I meant to say. You are reading into this all wrong. Please forget what I just said."

And now it is time for me to say goodbye to my brothers. This time it is very difficult. We all have so much on our minds based on the confession of our mom. I volunteer to drive Scott, Chuck, Randall, and Granada to the airport and when we hug each other goodbye, we hold on tight not wanting to let go.

"I love all of you, so please have a safe flight, and let's talk often. We all have so much to absorb, but the one thing that remains constant is Mom. We need to be here for her, and I know I can count on all of you. Susannah and I will keep you abreast of any information we find out about Dad. If any of this is true, all of us will be in for one big surprise."

Taking our mother's declining health into consideration, we know that we will be seeing each other very soon. But, more importantly, we recognize the urgency of contacting our father in September. We all agree that I will respond to our father's *New York Times* ad with an encrypted message 'sacrificed4utoolong' implying that the truth is out, along with Susannah's home address. Our hopes are that he will respond positively.

Chapter 12

Marcus, 27, Former Law Student

The room is pitch dark; the air conditioner is on high; soft music is playing in the background. Rina is lying on her back, knees spread apart, completely unclothed. Marcus, bare naked too, hovers over her body. Not being able to see anything but eager to touch, he begins to lightly caress her face with his fingertips, slowly and methodically touching every curve of her nose and her eyes; he hesitates at her mouth and gently brushes his fingers along her full lips. Tracing her slim, but muscled arms, to her palms to her wrists, Rina is panting, finding it hard to breathe.

Marcus' fingertips move down to her neck, her shoulders, and her breasts. He circles his fingers around her nipples, tugs gently, and moves down to her navel. This time he uses his tongue to circle slowly around her navel, and travels slowly down to her hips, to her thighs. Rina's inclination is to spread her knees even more as Marcus moves down between her legs, gently licking and kissing the inside of her thighs. A loud moan comes from Rina's mouth when Marcus begins to suck the moistened area, focusing on her erotic zone. Rina cannot stifle the sounds from her mouth anymore and screams out loud as she reaches a climax.

I wake up sweaty; haunted by the dream; disappointed that the woman next to me is not Rina, but Lisa.

I can't say that Lisa and I are not getting along, because we are. We enjoy each other's company, and we laugh a lot, but it's just that the relationship seems tense, to say the least. Both of us are trying so hard to please each other, but it all seems so forced, so desperately unnatural.

Of course, my work schedule does seem to put a damper on my relationship with Lisa. Since I haven't received the results of the California Bar exam yet, technically the firm that has offered me a permanent position, Copeland and Turner Entertainment, cannot hire me as an attorney until after

I pass the bar. But in the meantime, Copeland and Turner Entertainment has offered me an interim position on an hourly basis. As a result, I am putting in extremely long hours to make sure that Copeland and Turner Entertainment continue to be impressed by my notable work ethics. But Lisa has chosen to do the opposite. She decided to take a leave of absence from her job as an exotic dancer in order to spend valuable time with me.

When I return home late in the evening, I can see the disappointment in Lisa's eyes. Although we are not officially living together, she spends the majority of her time at my apartment rather than her own.

I know that my biggest problem is that I keep comparing my relationship with Lisa to Rina's relationship with her boyfriend. Although Lisa is warm, loving, exciting, and beautiful, something is missing. I want the all-consuming loving relationship that Rina has with her boyfriend. Accidentally witnessing their passion for each other a few month earlier makes my relationship with Lisa feel inadequate and shallow. And that is not fair to me, Lisa, and our relationship.

And the fact that I am having sexual dreams about Rina, doesn't help either. At night, my mind won't stop conjuring up Rina's face in my dreams. In those meager few months, we easily developed a unique relationship, with a block wall between us, and I miss her quick-witted, sassy attitude of righteousness when she tries to prove a point. Last time we spoke, we promised to keep in touch, and we have; via texting. Every once in a while, she will text me to ask how I am doing, inquire about my relationship with Lisa, and give me an update on her mother.

I know it won't be long before her mother passes away, and she will move back to New York to move on with her life, and to her boyfriend. This makes me sad that I may be losing the one person who gets me, but honestly, she was never mine to have. And that is why she haunts me in my dreams, and I know I need to do something about that.

The day has arrived, and the results are in. This is the moment all law students who have taken the bar have been waiting for. But, knowing that once the results have been announced online, it will be either good news or not. I am in my office with the door shut and the computer screen is displayed before me. All I have to do is push the return button and the results will appear.

I feel grateful that I am alone. This is one task that should be done with no one else around. For instance, what if the person you are with passes, and you don't, or vice versa? That would be an awkward moment.

My hands are shaking, and I know that I need to do this, but I am actually afraid for the first time in many years. I have dedicated the past three years to this exact moment. I push the button, but then I close my eyes. Willing them to open, I search for the results. And I passed.

Not five minutes after the results are posted, the receptionist from Copeland and Turner Entertainment calls me and informs me that the partners have summoned me to the firm's boardroom and could I get there as soon as possible. I nervously conjure up enough energy to walk down the hallway, into the boardroom. Shocked for sure, all five of the partners are standing in the middle of the room, holding a crystal champagne flute filled with bubbly liquid.

"Marcus, my man. Congratulations. We can officially welcome you as a new team member to Copeland and Turner Entertainment. Please take this glass and let's have a toast. To Marcus Spencer, may you never regret joining our firm and here's to your future here. We knew you could do this." It amazes me how fast good news travels.

After the initial celebration, they tell me that I am free to leave for the day but to report to the office Monday morning ready to begin a new chapter in my life. Walking back to my car, my first impulse is to call Peter, David, Aaron, Conner, and Blake, but when I glance at my phone, there is a text message from each of them informing me that they had passed the bar exam, too. Immediately, I text them back to let them know that I passed and ask them if we could all celebrate next Saturday night.

Then I call Rina; there is no answer, so I leave a message. After hanging up, I realize I should have called Lisa first, and I feel a little guilty. I leave a message on Lisa's phone, and within five minutes, my phone rings, and I recognize the caller to be Rina, not Lisa.

"Oh, Marcus, I am so happy for you. You need to celebrate." Happy that she made that suggestion, I ask her if she can meet me tonight for dinner.

There is a slight hesitation, and then she tells me that she is sure that there are more important people in my life to share this incredible news such as my parents and Lisa. She continues to tell me that she has never intended on joining the celebration. I laugh a bit embarrassed and tell her that I am definitely my parents' lowest priority, and I explain that they are not the type of parents that want to celebrate my successes. She is surprised by my honesty, but I manage to cheer her up and tell her that I was expecting a call from Lisa and hope to celebrate with her. But, to be honest, Rina is the only person I want to celebrate with, and I am more than confused by this revelation.

"Tell me, Marcus, what happens now that you passed the bar? Does it impact your status at the firm? Will they immediately see such value in you that they make you one of their partners?" It is obvious she is teasing me, but I enjoy answering her amusing questions.

"First of all, they gave me an enormous raise, six figures, which opens up a great opportunity for me to go out and buy a huge house, just like your sister's. Secondly, not only did they make me a partner, but they put my name first on all the stationery. The firm will now be known as Granger, Copeland and Turner Entertainment." Her laughter cheerfully resonates in my ears.

I finally hear from Lisa, and she agrees to meet me at the restaurant of my choice to celebrate. But, for some reason, I am not excited about the celebration, and this confuses me even more.

After several days of sulking, I finally decide to be proactive. I am going to visit Rina; to let her know that I think about her often and see how she responds to my words. Knocking on the enormous door of her sister's home, my palms all sweaty. I wish I could just walk away, but I can't. When the maid opens the door and sees me standing there, she smiles widely and begins to escort me to the kitchen, and I instantly stop walking as I overhear Rina's voice.

"The reality show "Love at First Sight" is such a farce that the producers actually pay the participants to stay together for at least three months. Once that time period is up, the couples will be paid a particular sum of money whether or not they stay together after that time. The ratings are based only on those first three months, which makes this show a total hoax." And then she laughs and claps her hands. "My editors love it."

'Hmmm' is the only sound I make.

Caught off guard by the sound, she turns and sees me standing there and begins to stumble. "Marcus, How... what... hi, so nice to see you."

"Don't give me that, Rina. We need to talk." Looking at her sister and mother, I mumble, "Excuse us." I take her hand and pull her out to the backyard with her protesting the entire time. Once we reach the gazebo, I release her hand and scowl at her.

"How can you do that to me? You know I trusted you and told you things about the show never knowing that you would betray me and our friendship. Do you want to know the reason I came over today? I wanted to tell you that I can't get you out of my head, both awake and asleep. You haunt me, I wanted to know if you are having the same thoughts. But you aren't, are you, Rina? You have made a laughing stock and a fool out of me."

"Do you know what can happen to me if the producers find out that I was the one to spill the beans about the details of the show? I can be sued or even worse, put in jail. I signed a confidentiality contract stating that I would never divulge the type of information that I just heard you read out loud. I know you told me once you were a writer for an entertainment magazine, but I didn't know that you felt so little about our friendship. How can you do this to me?"

Tears flow out of Rina's eyes. "Marcus, let me explain. I never intended to let on that you were the one to tell me the show's secrets. And, besides, you don't have to worry, the article hasn't been published yet. I can stop it right now. I will tell my office to destroy it. I am so sorry. Will you ever forgive me?"

"How can you ask me that, Rina? This is unforgivable. I thought you were a better person. Please forget you ever knew me. I would appreciate that consideration. Please do not try to contact me. Goodbye." And I walk away, never knowing what could have been.

Chapter 13

Rina Spencer, 27, Freelance Writer

Still sitting in the gazebo where Marcus accused me of betraying our friendship, I haven't stopped crying since Marcus walked away. I am so confused because I know that he is only a friend, nothing more, so why does this betrayal hurt so much? I am unable to face my sister and mother right now. Unsure of what my next steps should be, I have no energy to walk back to the house.

Frustrated on so many levels, I know I screwed up. Of course, I am not only upset about Marcus, but I am truly upset that I lost a good friend. Our friendship has so many levels to it, he was my confidante, my protector, and he truly got who I was and accepted all my faults, except for this one.

But right now, I cannot think of Marcus and what is lost, I have something else more pressing on my every thought. I am sad about losing a friend, but my finding out if my father is still alive has become a priority.

After sending an ad to our father in the *New York Times*, leaving a contact phone number and address, we have not heard one word from him, encrypted or other. Not knowing what else to do, Susannah and I are thinking of contacting a private eye specializing in missing persons, and it makes me realize the importance of this decision. We all need to find out the truth for our mother's sake, as well as ours even if we may be opening up an entire can of worms.

Admiring Alex's rational and unemotional advice, we ask him if he thinks we should hire a private eye detective to look into the death of our father. And he tells us to go forward with those plans.

We know that Frank's body was never found, so it sounds as if our efforts will be a complete waste of time, but what else can we do? Maybe we can get some closure to what happened that day. Obviously, we all need it.

The private eye's name is Mr. Canderfish, and for some reason, his name makes me laugh. Susannah tells me I am being silly, but instead of being offended, I laugh even louder.

Sitting across from Mr. Canderfish, I try hard to put on a serious face, which I find very difficult. First of all, he reminds me of one of the three stooges, probably because his hair is curly, black, and bald in the front. His round, pinkish face is smooth except for the deep wrinkles on his forehead. At 6'2" tall, one would expect a trim body, but not in his case. His shirt is pulling at the buttons by his expansive belly that presses against the edge of his desk.

Susannah gives me a look that says, 'Don't you dare laugh', which only makes me want to laugh out loud even more. As I sit here trying to keep a straight face, Susannah tells Mr. Canderfish our ridiculous situation.

"Nothing excites me more than the impossible challenge. I can contact the *New York Times* and use the tactic that the person in question has been missing for 18 years, and hopefully, they have a forwarding address on file that provides us with a lead as to the whereabouts of your father. Now since your father never responded to the ad from three weeks ago, there is a chance that what your mother told you may not be the truth. But, for now, let's not go in that direction." We agree that it sounds like a good plan.

Later that afternoon, it becomes apparent to both my sister and me that our mother is more than struggling today. She can't make up her mind what she wants to eat, so she eats nothing. She continually has a difficult time keeping her eyes open and insists that we bring her to bed so that she can lie down and rest. She no longer has control of her bowels, and that has become a nuisance to both my sister and me. In addition, bathing her has become an almost impossible task.

Lately, I have to get in the bathtub with her in order to keep her from slipping under the water while my sister tries to bathe her. Neither of us wants to think the worst, but the doctors have informed us that Mom can take a turn for the worse at any time. We both agree that it is time that we contact hospice and have them attend to our mom on a more than weekly basis.

I have lived with Susannah and Alex for almost six months, so it shouldn't be a surprise to any of us. In the beginning, we were told that our mother has about six months to live. So we are lucky that she has hung on this long. But, more importantly, Susannah wants Mom to meet little Frankie. Although

Susannah is due in two weeks, it is our hope that Mom hangs on until little Frankie is born. We are all keeping our fingers crossed.

Sitting outside, contemplating the fact that I will be losing my mother soon is heartbreaking. I feel alone and sad. Although I have no control over my mother's fate, after a few hours of feeling sorry for myself, I realize that I need to be proactive about what I can control. I am unable to remember the name of the entertainment law firm that Marcus is currently working at, a dozen web searches later, and I have conquered that challenge. I recognize the name Copeland and Turner Entertainment. I giggle to myself when I remember what he said after he passed the bar exam, that the firm changed their name to Granger, Copeland and Turner Entertainment. His humor always makes me laugh, and I miss that.

Showered, with hair washed and makeup meticulously applied, I realize that Marcus and I are not finished. I want to set the story straight. For some reason, I hope he allows me to apologize in order to rescue our friendship. I miss him and at least, I hope to get a chance to rectify our friendship.

Although I am used to the obnoxious traffic in New York, the option to take the subway is always the best choice. But not a choice in Los Angeles. Driving to downtown Los Angeles is a nightmare. Bumper-to-bumper traffic, with most drivers trying to cut you off just to get one car ahead. But I finally manage to find the high-rise building where Marcus works.

Walking up to the receptionist, trying to conjure up as much courage as I can, I ask to see Marcus Granger.

"One moment please, let me see if he is available. May I ask who is calling?"

"Yes, tell him, Rina Spencer."

Holding my breath, I can hear her tell him on the telephone that a Ms. Rina Spencer is here to see him. The receptionist hangs up and proceeds to tell me that he is not available at that moment.

Trying hard to remain calm, and holding my head up high, I smile and choke out the words, "Please call him back and tell him that this is very important and that I wouldn't have battled the god-awful downtown traffic just to see him if it wasn't."

Looking closely at me, it is obvious that she notices the tears beginning to swell up in my eyes. Giving me a look that says, *I understand,* she calls him back and says that Rina Spencer is on her way to see you in your office. I love girl power!

My legs are shaking as the receptionist escorts me down the hallway and stops at one of the smaller offices. Taking a deep breath, I open the door and slowly walk in.

The sound of the door opening and closing distracts him and when he looks up from some paperwork on his desk and sees me, I hear him say, "Rina, don't waste your time or mine anymore, just leave. We have nothing to discuss."

Not sure of what my plan is, but for some reason, seeing him sitting in such an official lawyerly manner, dressed in a white shirt and blue striped tie, looking so confidently handsome, I can't stop myself. I walk over to where he is sitting, I pull him up by his hands to a standing position. Now we are face to face, and I put both of my hands on each side of his face, I reach up on my tippy toes, plant my lips on his, and whisper, "You are wrong, Marcus; we are not over."

Immediately, an electrical current goes through my body, but at the same time, he is trying to pull away, murmuring incomprehensible words at first. But, at last, he breaks free.

"Stop it, Rina. This isn't going to work. What has come over you? I never took you for a tease." Walking over to the window, and refusing to turn around to look at me, he speaks words that are meant to hurt.

"Go home, Rina. There is nothing between us and there never will be. Do not humiliate yourself anymore. I know that you are too proud of a person to keep doing that. Let's end it right here. I don't ever want to see you again. Please leave, now!"

Speechless for once, which doesn't happen too often, I back up to the door, turn slowly and walk out. Leaning up against the closed door, I take a few gulps of air and try to compose myself. I am shocked by my aggressive behavior and am truly surprised that I felt such a strong connection when we kissed. Realizing that I probably appear ridiculously guilty standing in the hallway, I turn to leave, but a sense of pride and possibly stupidity passes through me, and I decide that he is wrong again, we are not done.

Opening the door, I march straight up to Marcus, who is now sitting back down at his desk once again. I lean across his desk so that I am so close I can hear his heavy breathing, look directly into his fiery blue eyes, and say, "No, Marcus, we are not finished. I know that I have damaged our friendship, but

I think we have more than just a friendship. I cannot explain it to myself, but I felt such a connection when we kissed, and even though I had no right to do that, I am glad that we did. And, for some reason, I can't let it go. Can you?"

Obviously struggling with his thoughts, it seems that hours are passing even though it has only been a few minutes. Marcus just stares at me with a cold, blank look. Finally, he manages to stand up, walks around his desk, grabs both of my hands, and says, "Well, Rina, I think we may have a problem." He smiles, exposing his very sexy dimples; pulls me into his arms; and begins to kiss me. The passion that swells up between us is obvious.

"Marcus…" Trying to push back, not sure if I am protesting or not, he cuts me off with another hard-bruising kiss. His mouth seduces mine expertly, parting my lips so that he can explore deeply and at his leisure. My response is one of pure pleasure. His mouth against mine is hard, soft, gentle, then demanding. I feel weak, limp, and totally conquered.

When we part, the confusion in my eyes gives him enormous pleasure, as I contemplate and try to control the rising emotions raging through my body.

Although it is difficult to say goodbye, I manage to walk out of his office without stumbling. Passing the receptionist, I smile and mouth the words, "Thank you." I feel elated knowing that my mission for today is accomplished. Totally immersed in guilty thoughts, I drive home on auto-pilot, not even aware of my surroundings or how I manage to get home safely. Heading straight to my room, I lie down on my bed, asking myself, *What do I do now?*

***

It isn't until the next morning that I fully realize the impossible situation I have put myself in. Knowing how much I have always relied on my sister's advice, I seek her out.

I find Susannah in the baby nursery, putting away some baby clothes she has ordered online. Unwrapping a pale, pink frilly dress, with matching socks and tiny little ballet shoes, I watched her eyes light up with joy. Trying not to startle her, I lightly tap on the door.

"Oh, Susannah, that is probably one of the most beautiful little dresses I have ever seen. You have such an incredible knack for choosing the perfect outfit for yourself, and now the baby. I can't wait to see her wear this particular one. She will be the best-dressed baby in this entire city."

Rubbing her swollen belly, and smiling, Susannah, who is very intuitive at all times, puts down the outfit and walks over to me. "Rina, I think it is time to talk about what is going on between you and Marcus. Don't think I haven't noticed, but I wanted you to figure things out on your own, without my interfering."

Trying not to cry, knowing I will not be able to stop the tears once they start, I let my sister lead me outside to the gazebo.

Once we are seated, I can tell she is waiting for me to begin.

With a big sigh, I pour out my heart.

"Susannah, I am in deep trouble. You know how much I love Brandon and that he is my whole world that is not the issue. But is it possible to love two men at the same time? I didn't mean for this to happen, but it did. There is something happening between Marcus and me, and I can't stop it even if I want to."

Pursing her lips, Susannah asks me if she can say something first before I continue. I tell her yes.

"I think that you are missing Brandon, probably even before you came out to California. Ever since Brandon started medical school and now his residency, you told me that you two spend more time apart than together. You feel lonely, and it is obvious to me that Marcus has helped to fill that void. Your emotions are in turmoil. You are transposing your feelings for Brandon onto Marcus. It happens, but it doesn't mean that what you are feeling is not real. I don't think you intend to be unfaithful to Brandon, but you do need to figure things out before it goes too far. What do you want to do?"

"I don't know. My thoughts are all over the place. I like Marcus a lot, more than I want to, but I am not sure what to do about those feelings. After I thought I managed to lose Marcus's friendship when he discovered that I was writing an article about the show, I was devastated and lost. I drove to his office yesterday, and we kissed. I felt such a strong physical connection, and it surprised me. Now I don't know what to do. I am so confused."

"Rina, it is not the end of the world, and you don't need to make any immediate decisions. If you want to continue seeing Marcus to figure out your relationship, I would encourage it. Kissing another person is not a betrayal, especially if you are confused. But I would recommend you not to take it any further than that. Can you fall in love with two men at the same time? Probably.

But I also know that you have to really concentrate on what is important to you. What makes you happy?"

Nodding my head and giving her a weak smile, I tell her that I will definitely take my time and not rush into any major decisions until I figure out what I want.

What I don't understand is why I have this special soulmate connection with two men. What is it about these men that has me confused? I always thought that Brandon is the only man for me, but what has changed? All I know is that I wish I didn't feel this way about Marcus, but I do, and I don't see that changing while I am still living in close proximity to him.

"It's natural, Rina, to be confused. I am not to say that you are cheating on Brandon, but you will figure it out in time. And in the meantime, don't fret about what happened today with you and Marcus, just focus on what makes you happy."

We hug and then walk back to the house, arm in arm. Small talks like these have always given me the strength and hope that is necessary to continue leading my life with confidence. Susannah has always been my sounding board, and I am so thankful that she is my older sister, albeit by five years. Our relationship became so much stronger during the September 11th tragedy, when we all had each other.

In the past, I would share these feelings with my mother, but she is no longer the person I can turn to. And this also makes me sad. I can't believe that I miss my mother, even though she is not gone yet. But, thankfully, I have Susannah.

Chapter 14

Marcus, 27, Former Law Student

After Rina walked out of my office, it was impossible to concentrate on the pile of case files on my desk. Rubbing my temples, trying to ease some of the tension that has built up from the moment that Rina walked through my office door, I cannot help myself from admiring her spunk when she walked back into the office after I sent her away. Even though I was serious and had convinced myself that I didn't ever want to see her again, that first kiss evidently changed my mind. I have never ever in my entire life felt such a passionately-filled kiss before or met a girl with such a gust for life. All my anger disappeared and then I felt nothing but desire.

I thought I hated her for what she did with the information I accidentally spilled about "Love at First Sight," I was so grateful when she walked away. But, when she came storming back in like a wild jaguar, her green eyes all ablaze, I knew I couldn't stop myself. I had to kiss her again, just to make sure. And, damn, it happened again. And I knew I had forgiven her. I couldn't care less about that reality show. I don't care if they sue me or not. And, especially, I do not want any of their money either.

But now I am in a very bad predicament. First, I don't really know where I stand with Rina. She has a live-in boyfriend and I have first-hand witnessed their passionate love for one another. And I am extremely jealous thinking about their relationship. What does she plan to do about that? But one thing I am sure of is that I don't want to be with Lisa. Our courtship or whatever you want to call it is over.

Tonight, Lisa and I have plans to meet for dinner at a posh sushi restaurant just down the street from my office. In a way, I feel sorry for Lisa. She is going to be totally blindsided, and it is definitely not fair. But it also isn't right for me to string her along any further. Lisa has so much to offer any guy, but I am not that guy. I am not her bachelor.

From the get-go, Lisa and I both knew that in order to make this relationship work, we both have to give it our all. I should have known from the beginning that it was not going to happen. Unfortunately, Rina had already wormed her way into my heart. Ever since I heard that false southern accent of hers, I couldn't help myself from seeking her out day in and day out. And the connection kept building.

Knowing how much I am dreading this inevitable conversation with Lisa, I can't stop noticing many male admirers' eyes following her as she walks into the sushi restaurant sashaying to the table only the way Lisa can. She is dressed in a simple black halter dress that hugs her incredibly curvy body like a glove.

Leaning over to softly kiss my lips, she then scoots over in the booth so that her long smooth legs are touching mine.

"Hi, handsome, how was your day?"

"Uneventful, to say the least. How was yours?"

"Well, you won't believe it, and I think you will be so proud of me. I interviewed for a real job."

Surprised by this admission, I find myself speechless.

"Yes, I can see you are surprised. I had lunch with an old college roommate, Miriam, and she is the one who told me about this position that is opening up with the company she works for. It is right up my alley with my degree as a psychologist. After much thought, I realize that it is time for me to put my dancing shoes to rest and try to become more acceptable as the girlfriend of a prestigious, reputable young lawyer. And, besides, I have no regrets being an exotic dancer; that choice did help me financially to get my degree to begin with."

Now I am still sitting here stunned as she continues to ramble on. She is so excited about her plans that she doesn't even realize that I haven't said a word in the last ten minutes. Finally, I see a puzzled look come across her face, making her normally perfect brows arch up.

"Marcus, what's going on? Am I talking too much? Did you have a difficult day at the office?"

Finally, finding my voice, I say, "Lisa, we need to talk."

My serious tone gets her attention, and she scoots away from me slightly.

"I am very happy that you are making changes in your life but don't do it for me, do it because it is what you want."

"Of course, this is what I want."

"Good, but I am not finished. We both knew that making this relationship work was going to take time and effort. Perhaps, it was the reality show or the fact that we really didn't know each other very well before we were thrown together as a couple. But, honestly, it is not working for me. I can't pretend anymore. I am sorry, Lisa, but it is over. I want out."

And my biggest mistake, at this moment, is looking at her face. I can tell she is in shock and not sure what to say next. Knowing how prideful this beautiful girl is, I cannot help but admire the way she is handling my abrupt, unexpected confession. I am impressed by how she responds. She quietly wiggles out of the booth, excuses herself from the table, and gracefully walks away, without giving me a second glance. That is one amazing girl, but unfortunately, not for me.

By the time I walk back into my apartment, I notice that there is not one item remaining that belongs to Lisa. Wasting no time, she must have rushed over here and packed all her clothes, cosmetics, and toiletries before I got home.

Laying in my bed later that night, I turn on the news to avoid thinking about Rina. I have no idea what will happen next between us, and it makes me nervous. Should I call her up and ask her on a date, or should I wait for her to make the next move? Closing my eyes while the television drones on, I slowly fall asleep looking forward to my next encounter with the dark-haired, head-strong girl who makes my heart beat to another tune.

Chapter 15

Rina Spencer, 27, Freelance Writer

Waking up the next morning, I roll out of bed, look in the bathroom vanity mirror, and shudder at the dark circles under my eyes. Obviously, I did not have a good night's rest as I intended when I went to bed at 8:30 pm last night. Checking my cell phone, I notice two missed calls from Brandon. Usually, we talk every night once he gets home, but last night, I put my phone on silent, not quite ready to talk to him. He has always been acute to my thinking, and I am not ready to talk to him because I know he will know that something is amiss.

Today, Susannah and I are taking our mother to the doctor to address her memory issues. She seems increasingly confused about her whereabouts and continually asks us if she can see Frank one last time before she dies. After that time when she confessed that Frank was still alive and that he did not die on September 11th, she rarely brings up Frank, which makes it difficult for us to know the truth. The day after her confession, all of us questioned her about what she had revealed to us, and she tells us she has no idea what we are talking about. Confused and relieved, we decide as a group that she has no idea what she tells us and that we should just let it go.

But Rose's mind seems to waiver and each day we have no idea what to expect. One day, Frank is still alive and the next day she announces that he died on September 11. On those days that she insists that Frank is still living, she asks Susannah and me if we tried to contact Frank in the New York Times. We always respond to that question, "Yes, we are trying Mom, and we put a coded message in the newspaper, and we are waiting to hear back from Frank."

But, with these memory losses, Susannah and I are not sure how to proceed so we decided to make an appointment for her to see the doctor, and perhaps he can help us with the diagnosis.

Sitting in the waiting room is always an embarrassing adventure when you are with your mother. Having no filters lately, she keeps talking out loud about each of the other patients waiting in the waiting room to see the doctor. It is very humiliating when our mother asks out loud if the fat person sitting next to her knows that it is unhealthy to be that fat and that they should go on a diet or if the bald man with a bandage on his head knows that he should change his dressing more frequently because she can see that it hasn't been changed in days. Both Susannah and I cringe the entire time, trying to distract her with one of the numerous magazines on the table.

Finally, we are called in to see the doctor, and we explain the memory loss issues that our mother is experiencing. He asks her several questions, such as 'Do you know what year this is? Can you count backward from 20 to 1?' Puzzling us, she successfully answers each question correctly. But, when he gives her three words and then asks her to repeat them a few minutes later, she is unable to. And, then when he asks her 'what is the date of her birthday?', she has no recollection. Nodding his head, and writing down some notes, he turns to us and tells us that he thinks the cancer cells have probably metastasized to her brain and is probably the reason for her sporadic memory loss and that it will continue to get worse as time passes.

We then share with him the drama with our father and how she keeps asking to see him. Not surprised at all, he tells us that is normal in this situation. But, before he finishes telling us what to expect, my mother pipes in.

"Don't think I can't hear you talk about me. How dare you insinuate that Frank is not alive. I spent two months searching for him in the debris and ashes after the terrorists drove the planes into the Twin Towers, but it was a waste of time for me. Frank intentionally disappeared that day to live with his other family. How can he do that to me or his children? It disgusts me that he played us for fools. He is not getting away with it. We have to find out if he is still alive and if he is, I want to tell to him face to face before I die that he is a cheater."

The look on Dr. Benson's face is priceless. Raising my eyebrows, I ask him if what our mom is saying could be the truth and tell him that her story changes from day to day about the whereabouts of our father and that we have no idea what the truth might be. Dr. Benson admits that he has no idea if it is or not, and unfortunately, deflates our hopes by telling us that there is no way to find out either. Susannah and I look at each other with genuine defeat reflecting across our faces, while Mom sits there with a smug look on her face as if she has a secret and won't share it with us. Reminds me of our ice cream shop trip and the tissue-tearing incident.

Later that night while I am getting ready for bed, I answer my cell phone when Brandon calls and I apologize for not picking up last night. Thankful for the distraction, I share with him the medical findings from the visit with the doctor today. I also tell him that due to our mother's insistence that our father is still alive, Susannah and I are hiring a private detective to investigate my father's death. Brandon tells me that he understands the stress that this has put on me, and he hears it in my voice.

Of course, he has no idea the stress I am dealing with, which not only includes my mother, but Marcus. We talk for several minutes, and when we say goodbye, I find it difficult to hang up the phone. Trying to shake it off, I lie down in my bed and slowly try to breathe normally and meditate.

The next day waking up, I feel refreshed. I jump out of bed, hop in the shower, and get dressed. Not sure where all this energy is coming from, I find myself sitting in the gazebo with a yummy croissant and espresso, waiting for my day to begin.

Chapter 16

Marcus, 27, Former Law Student

It has been days since Rina's visit to my office, and we both agreed that there is an unmistakable, undeniably eerie connection between us. But now I haven't heard one peep from her, and I am considering my options. Should I drop by or text her to say hello? Or should I physically call her up on the telephone? The first two options appear to be the easiest. This way, I am putting the choice in her hands for her to respond.

But, if she is as stubborn as I think she is, she might not respond and then, I am left with the last option, but by making that call, she also has the choice to not answer. It sounds like a no-win situation and is the main reason I hate dating. I never know what to do, and it is so frustrating.

Now that Lisa is no longer in the picture and my nights have been freed up, I have decided to put all my energy into the law firm. I intend to prove to the partners of Copeland and Turner Entertainment that they made the right choice to hire me.

But today is Saturday, and as is expected from an only son, I must rally up the courage to walk into the restaurant to have dinner with my adoring, loving parents. Ha!

I follow the hostess to the table at which my parents are already sitting, looking perturbed as if they have been waiting hours for me to arrive, their duplicate dirty martinis half-finished.

"Well, son," my father bellows in his familiar deep baritone voice, hoping to attract the attention of those dining. "I am glad you agreed to join us this time. It's time you filled us in on your future plans. We thought that you would bring that dancer girlfriend of yours so that we can meet her."

Leaning over to kiss my mother on her overly painted cheek, I reach out and shake my father's hand. The formality of our relationship is so stiff, it has to be obvious to those around us.

Once seated, I inform them that my position at Copeland and Turner Entertainment looks promising now that I passed the bar. Keen to my parents and how much they like to pry, I say nothing about the reality show or Lisa.

So unsurprising to me, my mom says, "But where is Lisa? Why didn't you bring her tonight?"

"Well, Mom that is because we are no longer dating. I have never believed in love at first sight or the entire concept of the show, so what else did I expect."

My father laughs, takes a sip of his martini, and continues to lecture me as usual.

"We agree, Marcus. I am glad you came to your senses. Who would expect a person to fall in love when the audience chooses the girl for you? Such insane stupidity. And, now at least, you can focus on your career instead of trying to make a relationship work. Knowing your priorities and following through is the only way to get ahead in this beastly world. Once you know that your career is stable and flourishing, then you can worry about finding a little lady to marry, but not until then."

Feeling the drain of this evening profoundly, I say, "That's right, Dad. Now can we please order so that I can get to bed at a decent time tonight." And the evening continues as I try hard to keep myself from pulling my teeth out.

Acting offended by my response, my father picks up the menu and instructs me to order the exquisitely, charbroiled rack of lamb with the grilled vegetables and wasabi mashed potatoes and tells me it will go well with the Montoya Cabernet he ordered.

After dinner, I quickly say my goodbyes, thankful to be finished with my monthly obligation.

Walking into my empty apartment, I realize how lonely my life has become. Tomorrow, ignoring my father's advice, I decide that it is time that I do something about it. Crawling into bed, with my mind made up on how to handle the Rina situation, I am anxious for daylight to arrive.

Now that morning has made its rude and blinding entrance, I no longer have the courage I had last night. Staring at my cell phone lying on the nightstand, I am hesitant to pick it up and make that call. I understand that Rina will have two choices, answer or ignore. Either way, I am screwed. If she answers, I don't know what to say and if she doesn't answer, I don't know if I should leave a message or just hang up. Like I said, either way, I am screwed.

Chapter 17

Rina Spencer, 27, Freelance Writer

When I listen to the voicemail, Marcus left on my cell phone this morning, it makes me happy that he has been thinking about me. He asked if we could meet up sometime today for coffee. I know really what he has in mind. He wants to delve into our so-called non-relationship. How can I tell him that I am not interested in him when actually I am?

I love Brandon. I don't love Marcus, but there is something sucking me into him like a Hoover vacuum. I have always enjoyed our conversations when he lived next door. Although he has consistently kept in touch with me since he moved away via text and phone calls, I never thought I would get involved with him in any other way besides as a friend. Do I want to see Marcus? Yes is the answer to that question. I also realize that I will be opening up a can of worms that does not need to be opened up.

I have so much going on right now that my life is complicated enough without adding Marcus to the equation. First and foremost, is my mother Rose. Her rapid decline seems to be happening overnight, but in reality, it has been obvious that the cancer is definitely progressively and aggressively bombarding her body and mind.

Now that we have called in hospice to monitor her every moment of life left, I should feel relieved. But I don't because I know what the end-all is, and it is tearing me apart knowing that she will not be a part of my life anymore. She won't see me get married, and she will never meet my children. Hopefully, in Susannah's case, she will succeed on both accounts.

The second task that needs to be tackled is the truth about my father, Frank.

Did he die on September 11, 2001? Thankfully, Mr. Canderfish is investigating that trail. He kindly calls every other night to give us an update on his progress which seems to be moving slower than a snail, if that is even possible.

Next is the delicate situation with my job or to be exact, my career with Lifestyles in NYC. I have been away from the office for more than four months, and even though I submit an article every month on various subjects from food, to entertainment, to celebrities, I understand their concern. Even as a freelance writer, your responsibility and obligation to the magazine is contractual. And, unfortunately, the articles I am writing are not worthy of publishing.

Even though they are aware of my complicated family situation, I am aware of my obligations. I have to admit I have been doing a shoddy job on my part. I only wish I could submit the one article that has taken up so much of my time. Exposing the truth about the ratings of "Love at First Sight" would have been a boost to both my career and the magazine. They are very upset with me over the fact that I canceled the publication of the article. My excuse is that the source I used does not give me permission to proceed, which is the truth if you think about it.

And, on top of all that, I have to deal with this mess I have let happen with Marcus and myself. I courageously texted him instead of calling him and agreed to meet him at a nearby coffee shop at 4:00 PM.

Walking into the coffee shop, I note that he is already seated, nervously fiddling with his cell phone, I battle the urge to turn around and bolt. But I don't.

"Hey, Marcus. How is it going?"

Smiling and once again exposing those sexy twin dimples, he stands up and pulls out the chair opposite him for me to sit, always the gentleman. That is one of his qualities that attracted me in the first place.

"Good to see you, Rina. What can I get you to drink?"

"How about a small iced latte?"

"Would you like anything to eat?"

"No, thank you. I am good for now."

Sitting here alone while he walks up to the cashier to order our drinks, I realize how easy it is to converse with him, even the small talk. There is no awkwardness at all. We have this comfort level similar to a relationship that has developed over time, like Brandon's and mine. And, in a way, it has emerged over time although we were not boyfriend and girlfriend, just friends. And perhaps that is just what we are, good friends who enjoy each other's company.

At least that is what I keep repeatedly reminding myself. I shyly glance over and evaluate this handsome man standing at the counter. Clothed in tight jeans that hug his firm bottom, I turn away, mentally slapping my face, upset about my observation.

Setting our drinks on the table, Marcus sits down and immediately says, "I have missed our covert meetings over the block wall. Just to let you know, Lisa and I are no longer dating. And I don't want you to feel guilty or responsible for the breakup. From the beginning, Lisa and I were not meant for each other, even though we did try our best, we ended it amicably. She is a great person, and I only want the best for her, and that is not me."

As Marcus is telling me about his breakup with Lisa, I wish I could give him some words of comfort. But I couldn't. When the show host first announced that the audience had matched Marcus with Lisa so long ago, deep down, it made me unhappy. It became obvious to my entire family that Marcus and I had a special bond. Now all I can do is sit silently as he continues.

"Two months had passed since we last saw each other across the block wall, and I thought I would never see you again. But seeing you walk into my office threw me off guard. For some reason when you came charging back into the office with such force and confidence, I melted. And, then when we kissed, I knew I couldn't let you walk back out that door not knowing our future. Where can we go from here? That is up to you and me to decide."

"I understand your situation with your boyfriend, but if for some reason you see yourself with me and not him, I am willing to see where this goes. I will not make any demands or pressure you to make a decision. Let's take this step forward one day at a time. Right now, my life is not as carefree as I would hope for. My career is my top priority, but I am willing to give it my all if you are willing to try, too."

I am tongue-tied and confused and begin to fidget in my seat during Marcus' announcement. Once we finish our coffee, he asks if we could go for a walk, I agree because I definitely need the fresh air to clear my thoughts. When he grabs my hand, I do not pull away. We walk around for a while and then he escorts me to my car. Shocking me, he leans in close and wraps his arms around my waist, and he places a tender kiss upon my lips. This time, although less desperate than that first time, the kiss erupts into a deep passionate sensation between us which causes both of us to back away.

"No," I cry out. "Why is this happening?"

"Yes," he corrects me. "You cannot pretend you don't want me as much as I want you. This doesn't happen every time; this connection between a man and a woman. What we have is special and unique, you cannot deny that."

"No," carefully backing away from him. "I never wanted this. This cannot happen again. Marcus, what am I supposed to do? A kiss should be a prelude, not an all-consuming force. I love Brandon, but I like you a lot, too. I don't think we should see each other. I have too much on my plate right now and any day my mother will die, and it is inevitable that I will have to face Brandon very soon. He knows me so well, there is no way I can hide my guilt."

"I am sorry, Rina. I never intended to put you in such a predicament. I know how I feel about you though, and I am willing to wait. Yes, I will wait, but I won't wait forever. And I hope I can give you the time you need to figure things out without pressuring you."

"I believe you, Marcus, but my thoughts are all over the place. One day I want to see you and then the next day, I think it is a mistake. We cannot have any physical contact until I know what I want. We can text and talk on the telephone, but nothing more. My brothers are coming into town tomorrow, and they will see right through me, too. I need to go, right now."

At a loss for words, I drive away, not knowing if I will ever see him again. Even though we started out as friends, it has developed into so much more. There is no denying that.

When I get home, the maid and Susannah are anxiously waiting in the kitchen for me. Susannah tells me that Rose refuses to get out of bed. We knew this day would come. Wanting to see for myself, we head to our mother's bedroom. Rose is lying so still, so tiny, like a child in the bed. We each take one of her hands and try to talk to her. She barely opens her eyes, and mumbles for us to let her be so that she can die in peace. The sadness in those once so lively blue eyes is heartbreaking.

"Mom," I say. "Why don't you let me get you a cup of hot tea and some toast? Can you sit up in bed so that you will be able to drink it? And while I go get your tea, Susannah will brush your hair. You always love to have your hair brushed." Now from past experiences, my mother can be extremely stubborn, and the energy she summons to give me such an evil look is surprising. Shaking her head, she then tells us that it is time to bring Frank to her.

"Mom, Dad is dead. That is something that I cannot undo, but I think it would be a good idea to call your sons. You have to keep your spirits, strength, and energy up until they get here. Can you do that for us?"

"No, I want to see Frank, only Frank." Susannah and I nod at each other. When my sister makes up her mind, there is no stopping her. We reach under Rose's arms, pull her to a semi-sitting position, and stuff two pillows behind her. I head out to the kitchen, while Susannah grabs the hairbrush on the vanity and begins to brush my mother's hair.

Once I head back into the bedroom, my mom is sitting up with a semi-smile on her face, eyes closed, while Susannah is counting the brush strokes as she brushes my mom's thinning hair. Little sighs escape from my mother's mouth.

My sister always gets the easy tasks and trying to get Rose to even take one bite of the buttered toast is a true challenge. But, at last, I succeed in getting her to eat a few bites of toast and several sips of tea. This entire activity takes about an hour, and now we can tell that Rose is entirely exhausted from the ordeal and immediately dozes off.

Once outside the bedroom, we make sure the twins are coming tomorrow as planned. Next on the to-do list, we contact hospice and explain the decline of Rose's health and ask them for 24-hour coverage. And, later that night, I inform Brandon that he also needs to be prepared to fly back to California.

Hospice shows up and tells my sister and I that it will be soon. They can't say exactly but at the most two weeks. This terrible feeling of death and doom overshadows the thought that our mother will die believing that her husband abandoned our family and is still alive. Even though we siblings made a choice to pursue this unacceptable mystery and have not made any progress, it doesn't make it easier on us. Rose believes that Frank is still alive and will die thinking that he is not a hero or one of the best men she will ever know.

I, for one, will not let her die thinking these horrible thoughts. It will be my mission that whenever she wakes up to remind her how she and Frank met, got married, and had a wonderful family and that he had died a hero trying to save others. When my brothers arrive tomorrow, I will insist that they do the same. Even if she never acknowledges the fact, she will hear us, and I pray, she will believe us.

It is obvious that Susannah is having the most difficult time knowing that my mother's life is near the end. Due any day with baby Frankie, it is all our wishes that my mom can at least meet the baby. After hospice leaves, Susannah tells me she needs to lie down and rest. The stress of this entire situation is not good for the baby, and I agree. Unable to call Brandon during the day, and needing some comfort and kind words, I call Marcus.

"Hi, Rina, I didn't expect to hear from you so soon since you told me before you left today that you need time."

"I know, Marcus, and I hate to intrude any further on your day off, but I need someone to talk to about my mom. My mother's health has declined to the extent that my sister and I called hospice today. They just told us that she will not be with us for much longer. You know I came here to spend these last months with my mom before she dies, but now that this time is near, I don't think I can do this. I am not ready to lose her."

"I am so sorry to hear about your mother, Rina. I recall the first time I met her and the way she took charge when you fell and hurt your ankle jogging. She was so full of life. I can't imagine what you are going through. Do you want me to come over?"

"No, I don't think that will be a good idea. Even though I told my sister about our situation, I don't think she will approve. I just wanted to hear your voice and talk about what is going on. I appreciate your thoughtfulness, and I am glad that we were able to meet up today." And then I unloaded the entire situation about my mom and her insistence that our father did not die on September 11, and her confusion about whether or not my father is alive living with another family. And then I told him how Susannah and I contacted a private eye to investigate the matter.

"Wow, you do have your hands full. What did the private investigator tell you?"

"Well, since we put in an ad in the New York Times, we still haven't heard anything from my father, not a phone call, ad, or even a letter. In the ad, we gave Susannah's address and phone number as contact information, but still no word. The private investigator doesn't sound promising. He tells us that he can try to trace the whereabouts of the person placing the personal ad, but he can't give us any guarantees."

"I am sorry to hear that. I, myself, would not know how to handle that situation either. Please, Rina, feel free to call me anytime you need to talk, OK. I am here for you. I have no experience in losing a parent, but you can always count on me to have a shoulder to lean on."

"Thanks, Marcus. I should probably go check on my mom right now. And, as I mentioned, my brothers will be flying in tomorrow. Just so you know, you might not be hearing from me for a while since I will be tied up with family matters."

"No problem. Please keep me informed of what happens. Talk to you later, Rina. Bye."

Chapter 18

Marcus, 27, Former Law Student

After hanging up with Rina, it occurs to me that her boyfriend will probably be flying in, too. And it bothers me to know her boyfriend is a vital part of her family dynamics, and I am not.

Calling up a local florist, I order a beautiful exotic plant to be delivered to the family of Rose Spencer, hoping that it will cheer them up. Next, I decide to contact a long-time friend of the family, a former CIA agent, who now specializes in missing persons, I know that if anyone can find out the truth, Thomas Abraham is the man. And, if Frank Spencer is still alive, I want to be the one to prove it. Rina told me that the family has hired a private investigator named Mr. Canderfish to help with the matter, but I thought of Thomas immediately when Rina told me the story.

"Hi, Marcus, good to hear from you. Of course, I can put out a few feelers to see what pops up on Frank Spencer. I know Canderfish very well, we have worked on a few cases together, and he is a good man. I will contact him and let him know that I am doing this as a favor for you, and perhaps we can work together to solve the mystery."

"Can you give me some background on his death and perhaps locations where Rose and Frank have been meeting on a yearly basis? Maybe they checked into hotels using his new name and that should give me a starting point. How are your dad and mom doing? I had dinner with them a few months back, but it's funny how fast time flies. Congratulations on passing the bar. You should be proud of your accomplishments. Thanks for calling, and I will keep you posted if I find anything. Bye."

Next, I decide to call up some of my buddies from law school. The long hours at our law firms prevent us from getting together often, but Sundays always seem to be a good time for all of us before our hectic work week begins.

Astounded by my break up with Lisa, the boys want the details.

"We were never compatible. Yes, Lisa has it all. She is Intelligent, sexy, beautiful; everything I want in a soulmate. And, even though we had chemistry, my heart was not in it. It is time to confide to all of you that during the taping of the show, I met someone."

"She is incredible, beautiful, sexy, smart and so much more. I was drawn to her the moment I saw her. Her laughter was so rich and attractive, that it caught my attention. At the time, she was living with her sister in the house adjacent to the bachelor pad. We accidentally met over a block wall, and I continued to visit with her several times throughout the taping of the show."

"We connected on so many levels, it is hard to believe. We met at a coffee shop this morning to talk about what lies ahead for us. Of course, as in most relationships, there are a few hiccups. First, she lives and works in New York, and is only here temporarily to be with her ailing mother, who is now unlikely to survive much longer. And, secondly, and probably my biggest hurdle, she has a live-in boyfriend."

After announcing the fact that she has a boyfriend, I can tell by the reaction of Peter and the rest of the gang, that this news is upsetting.

Peter jumps in first, as usual.

"Marcus, you have got to be kidding! A few hiccups! Dude, she is living with a guy. What makes you think that she will leave him and her job, for you? And I don't mean it in an insulting way. I am just surprised at the stupidity of what you may expect. What has she told you about her boyfriend that gives you the impression she will leave him? Wait, are you talking about Rina, the girl next door? Isn't she the one who tried to publish that article about "Love at First Sight" insinuating that the ratings are a fraud? You told us that you had nothing but contempt for her, and now you are telling us that you are in love with her."

"Yes, Peter, I think I am in love with her. I know this sounds ludicrous. But she is the one who contacted me after two months. She came to my office, and she kissed me. She made the first move. I didn't pursue her, she pursued me. And now I want to find out if we can be a couple. There is nothing wrong with that, is there? And besides, she never published that article because of me. That should tell you something about her character."

After defending myself and Rina, just like a great lawyer does, they all agree that I am crazy, but they wish me the best of luck. The rest of the afternoon, we spend telling funny work stories and how awesome it was that we all passed the bar exam. But, when you think about it, I am not surprised. We were all selected to be in a special group due to our intelligence, and we all studied together every day before the bar exam.

It doesn't make sense if one of us didn't pass and the others did. The six of us created a bond of friendship that I am thankful for every day, all because we got selected to be on a fast pass through law school. We were all thankful to be guinea pigs for the law school because it helped us form such a great friendship.

Rina and I talk daily now. She gives me updates on her mom, Rose, and I try to give her my support. I make extra efforts to keep our conversations positive and uplifting, knowing full well the strain she is under. In the background, I can hear loud boisterous voices, and I am happy that she is surrounded by her family during this difficult time. I only wish that I could offer more than just emotional support, but I understand her predicament.

Chapter 19

Rina Spencer, 27, Freelance Writer

Today starts out like every other day. As has become our daily ritual, my brothers, my sister, and I sit with our mother reminiscing about our happy, carefree childhood days when my father was still alive. Sometimes we play word games, and the laughter that bellows throughout the house is deafening. Rose lies there, most of the time with her eyes closed, but we know she is listening, especially when a small smile plays along her lips every now and then.

Brandon is coming in today, and I am excited to see him although the reason for him being here is obvious. As I was freshening up to drive to the airport, I hear a shriek, and then loud footsteps pounding up the stairs. Running out of my bathroom to check on the commotion, I see Susannah standing in the middle of the hallway, with a look of horror on her face.

"I think I just wet my pants," she cries out. About that time, both Scott and Randall arrive breathlessly and begin to laugh.

"Oh, Susannah, you are silly," I say. "You haven't wet your pants, your water just broke. You are going to have a baby today".

Susannah immediately smiles and tells us to call Alex and have him meet her at the hospital. We all agree to rendezvous at the hospital after I pick up Brandon, and Scott and Randall, Chuck and Grenada will drive Susannah.

Rushing around trying to get Susannah out of the house, and me on my way, it finally occurs to me that we have not thought about our mother.

"What should we do about Mom?" I ask.

Randall answers quickly, "She is in no condition to go with us. Hospice is here, there is no need to disturb her by bringing her to the hospital. She will meet Frankie when the baby comes home."

Once Randall says that, we all stop what we are doing and look at each other. I can't help myself, so I ask, "What if it is too late? What if she dies before Frankie comes home?"

None of us know how to answer that question.

Driving back from the airport, I tell Brandon all that has been going on and inform him we are going straight to the hospital.

"Rina, I think you are making a mistake leaving your mother at home. Make me responsible for her. I will wrap her up and take care of her. After all, I am a doctor, and I can handle any emergency situation that arises."

This is the reason why I love Brandon so much. He is so sensible, sweet, and always thinks of others first.

Of course, trying to bundle Rose up and put her in the car so that she is comfortable is a challenge. It surprises me that she has the energy to resist our efforts, but she does. Once we finally get her in the back seat lying down, I call my brothers to let them know we are on our way. They tell me that Susannah is doing fine, but the doctors tell them that this may take a while considering it is her first birth, which only makes me wonder if we have made the right decision to bring Rose. But, after thinking about it, what better place for her to be than at the hospital?

The looks that crossed my brothers' faces when Brandon and I came strolling through the hospital corridor, with Rose in tow in a wheelchair, made me smile.

"Yep," I say. "Mom deserves to be here just as much as us and there is no one more qualified to take care of her than Brandon." They didn't say one word after that comment.

After 10 hours of labor and all of us lounging in the waiting room, surrounded by scattered coffee cups and candy wrappers, baby Frankie is born.

"6lbs, 14oz," Alex proudly announces, walking up to us, completely disheveled and tired-looking but spouting a huge smile. He also informs us that Frankie has the lungs of a lion, just like his mother. This makes us all laugh.

Shaking my mother's shoulder, trying to arouse her to give her the good news, she awakes perky and alert, which surprises us all and mutters, "It's about time, now when I am going to lay my eyes on this beauty?" For a moment, we are stunned that she is aware of her surroundings, but then I remind myself that this type of behavior is normal. A dying person will have a second wind and appear to be normal, but it is just a temporary situation. And we are thankful that this is the moment for this behavior to occur.

Due to Alex's insistence, and I am sure of his agreement to donate money to the maternity ward, we are escorted to an enormous private room in order to accommodate our huge family. And Susannah is sitting up looking radiant as all new moms do, holding baby Frankie in her arms.

Scott and Randall return from their errand with pizza and bottles of wine, we shut the hospital door and celebrate. Rose is more awake than usual and when baby Frankie is placed in her arms, of course with the help of Alex, my heart melts. Kissing the baby on the top of her head, my mother tells us that she looks exactly like Susannah did when she was born.

One mission accomplished, my mom got to meet Frankie Rose. And it makes me happy that we are all together to share this momentous time with our mom, Susannah, and the baby. But it has been a long, long day, and it is time to kiss Susannah and the baby goodbye, and we all head home.

Once home, Brandon and I remain in the kitchen and decide to make decaf cappuccinos and spend some alone time together. Randall, Scott, Chuck, and Grenada plan to watch a movie on Netflix in the home theater room. And Alex immediately goes straight to bed. The strain of seeing his wife go through such an ordeal as delivering a baby took its toll on him.

Coming up behind me while I am preparing our drinks, Brandon wraps his arms around me and kisses the top of my head.

"I have missed you. I never thought that you would be away this long. How long do you think before you come back to New York?"

"Hmmm... good question. Once my mom passes away and Susannah is situated with the baby, I will come home immediately. No need to stay here any longer than necessary." After I say these words, my mind wanders off-track and Marcus appears in my thoughts.

"Why is your body shaking?" Brandon asks. "Are you okay?"

"Yes, I mean no," I immediately say.

"It's just that I am not ready to lose my mom." Thankful that I don't have to express another reason for my body's betrayal.

"I know, Rina. I will miss her, too. Let's finish our coffees and go back to your bedroom. I think you need some TLC, and I am the right person for that."

Chapter 20

Marcus, 27, Former Law Student

Work has been busy as ever, and I am not surprised that my caseload has more than tripled. With no personal life and little contact with Rina, it is a good distraction, though.

Yesterday, I had a late dinner with Thomas Baldwin and Mr. Canderfish. They have been working together to solve the case of Mr. Frank Spencer aka unknown and have made some headway in identifying a couple at a non-descript inn in Smith Rock State Park, Oregon that matches the description of Rose and Frank.

Thomas fills me in.

"It is obvious that credit cards were not used in order to avoid a paper trail. But this new lead is a positive one. It means that Frank Spencer aka unknown is still alive. Mr. Canderfish is meeting the family tomorrow to tell them the good news. I have to tell you that even though we know that Frank is still alive, it may be impossible to find him. But at least the family will know some of the truth."

After I get home that night, I want to call Rina and tell her the news. But I know it is not my place. So, instead, I open the freezer and pull out a carton of my favorite ice cream, mint chocolate chip, and eat its entirety, which only makes me even more anxious to call Rina.

Chapter 21

Rina Spencer, 27, Freelance Writer

Susannah and the baby are coming home from the hospital today and there is excited anticipation in the air. The maid is sashaying around the house humming a lullaby making sure that the house is spotless, which is ridiculous to think it is anything but clean.

Rose has been bathed and is more alert than normal, sitting in the kitchen in her wheelchair, anxiously waiting for the arrival of her daughter and new granddaughter.

Scott, Randall, Grenada, and Chuck decide to run to the market to buy a meal fit for a king or, in Susannah's case, a queen. Alex has taken the day off and has rushed to the hospital in order to bring home his new family.

Once Susannah and the baby are ushered into the house, excited chaos begins. Everyone is talking at once, an abundant spread of ham, turkey, roast beef, assorted cheeses, and breads is being served, while the baby just sleeps peacefully in her cradle.

Unaccustomed to visitors in the house, when the doorbell rings, we almost do not hear it. But, when the maid escorts Mr. Canderfish to the kitchen, we are anxious to hear what he has to say.

The news from Mr. Canderfish is very surprising to all of us. It confirms that our father never died on September 11. Not sure how we feel about this, we decide to approach our mother with the news who sat there the entire time Mr. Canderfish was speaking with her eyes closed.

We explain to her that we know Dad did not die on September 11 and ask her to please fill in all the details. Not wanting to articulate her thoughts, she continues to sit there with her eyes closed. I swear I can see her eyes flutter; she is intentionally trying to make us think that she is asleep. Susannah is the first to talk.

"Mom, I know we have to forgive you for keeping this to yourself, but right now, we can't. You kept our father from us and let us think that he was dead. We had a right to know the truth. You could have trusted us with that information, but you didn't. It was a selfish move on your part, and don't think that we are going to let this go. When you feel up to it, please talk to us about it."

Slowly, she opens her eyes, looks at each of us, and whispers, "I am sorry, and I have something to share with each of you."

"I have a journal of each time I met with your father, and I want to share that with all of you before I die. Susannah, could you please go to my bedroom and pull out the small red notebook in the top drawer of the nightstand and bring it to me?"

Dumfounded looks all around because we can all remember asking if she had any written proof, and she said no. Susannah returns with the notebook and hands it to our mother. She pulls out a piece of paper and reads to us.

Rose Spencer, my journal
September 11, 2001

I wake up in the morning like any other day. My usual routine involves waking all my children up to get ready for school at 7:00 am. Susannah and Rina, my two teenagers, are easy, but the eight-year old twins are a handful. First, it is like trying to move a mac truck to get them out of bed. Next, I have to sit on their bed as they disagree with the clothes I have laid out for them.

Randall always wants to wear the same old stinky, ratty Superman T-shirt that he has somehow tricked me into wearing every day for the last week. And Scott has a hard time figuring out why I won't let him wear a striped T-shirt with plaid pajama bottoms. Once that battle is over, I have to convince them that neither of them has more cheerios than the other when I set out their bowls of cereal.

Thankfully, Susannah has just gotten her driver's license and has agreed to drop off the boys every day for school as long as I allow her to stay out until 12:00 am on weekend nights. Why one hour is going to make any difference, I don't get it. And I keep reminding her that nothing good happens after midnight so that is the time we both agreed upon.

Once the children are out of the house at 8:00 am, I use that time to make beds, clean the kitchen, do laundry if needed, and then run errands. Today one of my errands was to vote in the primary elections which required me to drive into Manhattan across the Brooklyn Bridge. Pulling out of my driveway, I look around, I see several people walking outside, and I don't blame them because it was a beautiful, warm, sunny fall day (which cheered me up). I love these mornings. Just as I reached the Brooklyn Bridge, a low flying plane appears out of nowhere. It is flying so fast that I think to myself, 'Where do you think you are going buster'?

Suddenly, I feel my body jerk so hard in my car and all the cars ahead of me have come to a full stop. For a second, I assume that I am in a multiple car accident and someone has hit me from behind. Not sure what to do, I sit stunned, roll down my window to clear my mind, and realize everyone is getting out of their cars. Then I hear a loud, blood-curdling scream. Everyone is looking up at the sky.

I step out of my car and as I look up, I watch a plane hit one of the Twin Towers of the World Trade Center. My heart stops or at least I feel as though it is no longer beating. The blast was so intense and loud, that I could feel the Brooklyn Bridge shimmy and shake from the impact. My first instinct is to run toward the World Trade Center to help those who need help. But there were so many cars and people on the Brooklyn Bridge that I knew I would never get there in time.

I found out sometime later that what I saw was a second plane that hit the South Tower and the first enormous blast that I felt in my car was a plane that crashed into the North Tower. Smoke is billowing out from both towers now and black, sooty ashes begin to fall all around us as if God has turned on a fan near a major forest fire.

I am so numb I don't even know how much time has elapsed before I can move at all. Cars are backed up for miles and trying to move forward was impossible. All I want to do is turn around and head toward my children's schools. My mind keeps thinking, What if this attack is not only on the World Trade Center but happening everywhere? *My first thought is to get to the children. It never even occurred to me at the time to wonder how this attack would affect my husband, Frank.*

Finally, once arriving at the elementary school, I had a difficult time finding a place to park. Obviously, most parents had the same idea in mind. A mother's most important job is to protect their children and keep them safe. For some reason, the school made it very difficult to release students to their parents but after hearing the uproar from the hundreds of parents in the waiting line, the school relented. I stood in line outside the school office for two excruciating hours before I could put my arms around my beautiful boys.

The next stop is the middle school to pick up Rina which turned out to be much easier. I called the school office and had them bring Rina to the office for me to pick her up. Next was the high school, and usually, the school doesn't allow cellphone use during school hours, but today is an exception. I find Susannah crying in a corner with some other girls in the school office which is chaotic and hectic, to say the least. Once back to the car, I pull each of my children out of the car and into my arms, and we all cry together, me, Rina, Susannah, Randall, and Scott. It is a very unforgettable memory in my now diseased mind.

Traffic is horrendous, so I use the slow-moving traffic to call Frank to get some answers, but I do not have any cell phone service. Once I get home, I try calling Frank on the landline at his station, but I do not get any response. This has me somewhat worried, but knowing Frank, he is so busy taking care of the fires that he doesn't think to answer his phone, and perhaps the phone lines are down too. Wanting to turn on the news to get the latest update on the twin towers, I decide to shield the boys further from this moment. I send the boys to their rooms to play on their play station, which makes them happy as they skip away to their room.

The girls and I gather by the television, and we listen to what has happened this fateful day. To our horror and shock, we find out that both towers have collapsed, a plane has crashed into the Pentagon and a plane has crashed in some remote field in Pennsylvania (terrorist correlation has not been verified) and that thousands and thousands of people are either dead or missing at the World Trade Center. The word 'terrorist attack' has us all in panic mode. With still no word from Frank, I panic even more when I realize that many firemen and policemen were among the first responders. Not wanting the girls to realize that fact, I decide to turn off the television and suggest we sit and talk about how they are feeling about this sad event. I wanted to make them feel safe and secure, even though none of us admit to how scared we all are.

Once I realize that I have not heard from Frank, horror and reality jolt me awake. And what I do next is mainly responsible for this evil cancer. Frank is missing, and I spend almost two months searching through the sooty debris of twisted metal, broken concrete, ashes, burned clothing, and empty shoes at Ground Zero.

I never stopped hoping and praying, even though I was exhausted to the bone. It was as if the children didn't matter and my sole purpose in life was to find out what happened to Frank. And, then one day, I receive an anonymous voicemail on our home phone telling me to call an unidentified number. My first thought is that it is one of those annoying sales calls, but after a few days, I think to myself, What if it has something to do with Frank? Maybe someone found Frank, and he has no memory, and they located me through his New York driver's license. *So, out of utter desperation and sheer luck, I make the call and to my surprise and complete shock, I hear his voice, and the words he uttered are etched in my mind forever, "My dear Rose, I am alive, but I have to ask you a big favor. No one can know I survived the September 11 attack." After hearing those words, I fainted.*

It took me several minutes to regain my senses, and I called back the number. Frank reminded me all about the Conicci family and his involvement as an eyewitness to a murder. The plan was for him to testify as an eyewitness against the Conicci family, and then the government was going to enroll our entire family into the witness protection program. But September 11 proposed an alternate plan, and he made this decision quickly without much thought of what it would do to his family. He made a big sacrifice and chose to fake his death to save his own family.

At first, I was very, very angry and refused to listen anymore. I probably hung up on him a hundred times, but each time I managed to call him back once I calmed down. He kept asking me to keep this quiet from his children and everybody else. How can someone ask that of someone they love? I hated him and then loved him for what he was asking. It wasn't an easy decision on both of our parts.

After much discussion and coaxing by him, we made some choices that would affect my family's lives forever. We agreed to meet once a year, length and location to be determined. He will remain dead to everyone but me. Understand that this decision was not easy, but my love for your father made me live a lie for the rest of my life. From that moment on, I quit searching for him in the Trade Center remains.

I felt I was losing my mind during those first two months at Ground Zero. And now I was losing my sanity again. I struggled and had difficulty sleeping at night trying to figure out how I was going to keep these lies from my children. But thankfully, my grief was real. I didn't have to pretend that I was grieving because I was grieving over many things: the loss of our family unit, the loss of Frank unable to be with his children even though he was alive, and the fact that I had to be strong for the kids and prepare a life without Frank. My decision to go into nursing was easy. It gave me a purpose to help others.

June 2002
The Fingers Lake, New York

Frank and I are together for the first time since that fateful day. The only contact I have with him is via newspaper. He puts an ad in the New York Times explaining his whereabouts in code. Last month he asked me to meet him for one week in Finger Lakes, NY. This is where your father and I discussed our future, and it is decided that we will meet once a year for two weeks in different locations.

His whereabouts are to remain a secret from everyone I know. I explained to you children that in order for me to make peace with the fact that your father is gone, every year, I will be going on a retreat for two weeks with the church. And I decided at that time to begin a journal of my adventures with your father, never knowing if I would be able to share these memories with you.

June 2003
Baxter State Park, Millinocket, Maine

I am worried again for many reasons to see Frank but mainly I am concerned about his safety from the Conicci family. I can't help but look behind me when I am at the airport to see if anyone is watching or following me.

Once I get to the inn at Baxter Park, Frank is waiting for me in the lobby with open arms. He picked me up and swung me around, planting a huge kiss on my lips. I was ecstatic, almost like a teenager sneaking out to meet up with her boyfriend behind her parents' back, except for me it was my children which is another reason for my nervous concern. It was a lot of work just trying to plan out this two-week church retreat. Organizing school drop-offs and pick-ups for after-school activities requires much organization. Thankfully Susannah has her driver's license and is a huge help in most situations.

These two weeks have given both Frank and me a chance to reconnect on so many levels. Even though we never want to leave the comfort of our quaint little room with room service just a phone call away, we did find time to walk through many of the nature trails throughout the State Park although I did feel safer inside our room, away from peering eyes. Two weeks passed so quickly, and when it came time to say goodbye, we both agreed that 'goodbye' is not permitted in our vocabulary, and we decided to use the term from one of our favorite all-time movies, Same Time, Next Year. Parting was bittersweet but knowing that I would see him next year, made the emptiness that I felt much easier.

June 2004
Fredricksburg, Texas

Considered one of the prettiest towns in Texas, Fredricksburg is a charming small town with a Texas heart and German soul. We were registered at one of the romantic Bed and Breakfast Inns and feasted on fine wine and fine food and went to several festivals. We biked down picturesque country roads and strolled down the historic Main Street. I felt more comfortable in this small town and didn't feel the need to hide in our room.

Seeing Frank again has made me realize how much I miss him throughout the year, but I am grateful for the two weeks that we spend together. We never stop talking when we are out to dinner or just strolling hand-in-hand along the downtown streets. I recite stories about the family, along with recent photos so he feels that he is a part of their life. He always assures me that he made the right choice in order to save our family although I know that it is very difficult for him to admit that he may have been wrong. Same Time, Next Year.

June 2005
Block Island, Rhode Island

Block Island is a small island 12 miles off of the southern shore of Rhode Island, uncluttered and free of commercialism. Famous for unique lighthouses, and quiet sandy beaches, Frank and I explored this peaceful island as though we were trying to fulfill a lifelong prophecy. We loved every inch of this island and felt the safety of the tranquil island as it welcomed us. Same Time, Next Year.

June 2006
Smith Rock State Park, Oregon

    Smith Rock State Park is located in central Oregon's High Desert. Although Frank and I decide not to do any rock climbing, the scenic views of the cliff rock formations are incredible. We spend more time in our room this time, but it doesn't matter what state or city we are in; we are happy as long as we are together. Anytime spent with Frank is worth so much to me and waiting an entire year to have him near is not easy. Same Time, Next Year.

June 2007
Mackinac Island, Michigan

    What a lovely island where motorized vehicles are prohibited. Frank and I took the ferry across to the island from Mackinac City, and we stayed at a historic bed and breakfast Victorian-style home. The first activity we decided to do was ride a tandem bicycle around the eight-mile-long island. This gave us an opportunity to explore areas we would like to revisit. Known for their Mackinac Island fudge, we indulged daily in every flavor they made. Our time together here felt like it stood still and the love I felt for Frank intensified by the day. Same Time, Next Year.

June 2008
Devils Tower, Wyoming

    As our intentions were to visit sites and cities that were more remote than populated, this particular adventure was to see the Devil's Tower in northeastern Wyoming. Devils Tower is a butte composed of igneous rock. Our choice to go the first two weeks of June each year is to avoid the onslaught of summer vacations, trips, etc. with families. We prefer to be less noticed, and as invisible as possible. So far, Frank and I have managed to do that although at times we recognize that crowds do help us to blend in instead of standing out. Same Time, Next Year.

June 2009
Leavenworth, Washington

I love this city because it can be described as a mountain town that looks like it belongs in the Bavarian Alps. This German-inspired village is located in the Cascade Mountains in Central Washington and the beer, brats, and schnitzel were fabulous. For your father's safety, we are unable to travel internationally so this town made me feel as though we were in Germany. Same Time, Next Year.

June 2010
Woodstock, Vermont

Woodstock is a picturesque New England Village located in east-central Vermont. My favorite pastime was to walk hand-in-hand every morning with Frank across the covered bridge located right smack in the center of town. One of our most unusual outings was when we went to the Sugarbush Farm and tasted 14 varieties of cheese and maple syrup... a very interesting combination. Frank always keeps me laughing, and this adventure was no exception. Same Time, Next Year.

June 2011
Jekyll Island, Georgia

With 10 miles of sandy beaches, Frank and I enjoyed our evening strolls along the water's edge. Jekyll Island is a Georgia State Park and is renowned for its charm and tranquil scenic beauty left undisturbed by the constant march of time. So much to see, and so little time. Same Time, Next Year.

June 2012
Sedona, Arizona

Surrounded by red-rock buttes, steep canyon walls, and pine forests, Sedona is considered, in my opinion, one of the most beautiful cities to see. Also, being so close to the Grand Canyon, Frank and I set up a day trip excursion to see the magnificent canyon. Both locations became one of my favorites. If Las Vegas wasn't so crowded with tourists, but with the minute chance that we might run into someone we know, we decided against going there. Same Time, Next year.

June 2013
Savannah, Georgia

Known for its manicured parks, cobble-stone squares, antebellum architecture, and horse-drawn carriages, Savannah is a charming southern escape known for its haunted stories and Spanish moss. Frank and I compare Savannah to be reminiscent of the southern lifestyle in Gone with the Wind. It brought me back to those days, so I would have to consider Savannah my favorite of all the places that Frank and I visited so far and no doubt, Gone with the Wind is my favorite book and movie of all time. Same Time, Next Year.

June 2014
Amelia Island, Florida

One of the chain barrier islands that stretch along the east coast from South Carolina to Florida, Amelia Island is renowned for its crystal-clear water and pristine sandy beaches. 13 miles long and 4 miles wide. We stayed in the Fernandina Beach district and enjoyed a sunset boat cruise and a kayak excursion. The village is poster-perfect with rows and rows of antique and collectible shops which made me realize how much I missed perusing antique shops with Frank. My favorite part of this trip was when we went on a sightseeing river cruise to just enjoy the peacefulness of floating down a river. Same Time, Next Year.

June 2015
Ashville, North Carolina

A mountain city in western North Carolina, located in the Blue Ridge Mountains, Ashville is a beautiful city to visit. Frank and I enjoyed the uniqueness of this historic city and even went on a ghost tour, which was scary and informative at the same time. After that tour, we both looked at each other and agreed that there are some forms of ghosts all around us, all the time. This made us both laugh until tears were running down our eyes. Same Time, Next Year.

June 2016
Chatham, MA

Chatham is a seaside town at the southwestern tip of Cape Cod. With its adorable New England charm, Frank and I enjoyed the fresh seafood and our walks down Main Street. One night we over-indulged ourselves with lobster, crab, and mussels. The next day neither of us wanted to set eyes upon any type of shellfish so we opted for a good old-fashioned cheeseburger and fries for dinner. Same Time, Next Year.

June 2017
Sonoma, CA

Sonoma is located in the North Bay region of the San Francisco Bay area and is one of the principal cities of California's wine country. We stayed at a beautiful bed and breakfast inn and enjoyed many tours of the fine wineries. Since Sonoma is only one hour from San Francisco, we rented a car and enjoyed the sights and sounds of San Francisco. Madame Tussauds Wax Museum at Fisherman's Wharf is one of our favorite outings on this trip. Same Time, Next Year.

June 2018
Hilton Head, NC

One of the other barrier islands is very similar to Amelia Island, but more populated. We enjoyed the beautiful sandy beaches and the most wonderful restaurants. Frank talked me into taking a golf lesson. We both were not very good at the game, and we decided that golf wasn't our thing. We had a peaceful, lovely time just enjoying all the sights. Same Time, Next Year.

***

After effortlessly reading out loud the entire journal, she hands Susannah a letter that is worn on all the edges, as if it has been reread over and over. She then closes her eyes and waves her hand toward her bedroom insisting that we take her there. End of conversation. We all sat there stunned and her attitude when she was reading her journal gave us the impression that she was not lying and here is the proof. Mr. Canderfish had no words to say, so kindly left.

112

Now, all of us are staring at the letter in Susannah's shaking hand. We all are in shock by what just transpired, and this letter is one more stressful item to absorb. Susannah begins to read it aloud...

Dear Susannah, Rina, Randall, and Scott,

If you are reading this letter, I have to assume that your mother gave it to you and hopefully, you know the truth about my faked death. There are many reasons for choosing to take the path that I did, but it doesn't excuse the fact that I left all of you behind, and I will always regret that decision.

I loved each of you since the day you were born, and I have never forgotten each and every one of you since that fateful day, September 11. My heart breaks every day knowing the fact that I will never get to hug or kiss you again. But your mother and I agreed together on this decision in order to keep you children safe.

Every year, your mother and I have met for two weeks in the most remote places you can imagine. It is during one of these trips that we both decided to write a letter to all of you, explaining our selfish but necessary decision to keep you children in the dark about my death. As you probably know, your mother is a very stubborn woman, and it took a few years for me to convince her that it is the right choice to keep my existence a secret. The tears that flowed on both of our parts were enough to fill the entire Mississippi River. OK, maybe I am exaggerating just a little, but I want you to know how much this decision weighed heavily on our hearts.

But thanks to your mother, whenever we would meet, she would always bring videos and photos of your entire year of life. I watched each of you attend dances, play baseball, cheer, and graduate from high school and then college, and I am so proud of who you all have become. Obviously, I give credit to your mother as well, for supporting you and creating the beautiful people that you are.

I am not asking for your forgiveness. All I want is for you each to understand the decision that was made so long ago to keep you safe. My heart is overflowing with love for each of you, and I will love you forever and ever. Your father, Frank

After Susannah finished reading the letter from our father, there was not a dry eye in the room. We were numb to finding out the truth about that day from our mother and literally mentally exhausted after hearing our father's words.

As was evident the next morning by our haunted eyes with black circles beneath them, none of us had a good night's rest. We were blindsided and felt totally cheated and exploited by our own parents. Rose is stubborn, as our father noted, and we all have witnessed many times and has refused to make any more comments about Frank, the journal, or the letter. She stays in her room with her eyes shut and her mouth closed. We were all surprised yesterday how alert she was when she was reading her journal aloud, since earlier that day it seemed as though she was not going to make it through the night.

But this morning, Rose has returned to her catatonic self and does not seem to be aware of her surroundings, least of us all. After talking to the hospice nurse, about Rose's bout of energy yesterday, she mentioned that this type of behavior is common for someone who is dying.

We are not even sure she remembers what she shared with us yesterday, but we are constantly reminding her that we are not upset with her for her choices, but we are sad that we were kept in the dark about her escapades with our father and the fact that he was alive.

We also felt ashamed that we were so wrapped up in our own lives; we never asked her about her two-week travels, which we thought were with the church. We realize how difficult it must have been for her to keep everything a secret. Her life has not been easy either and as her children, we should have been more involved in her life.

But today, all of us feel as though we are falling through an abyss.

***

Four days later, the excitement and commotion of having a newborn around, has died down. Baby Frankie has brought a sense of happiness to us, that no one expected.

Just after breakfast, there is a knock on our door. The maid is the first to answer, recognizes Marcus, and calls my name.

"Rina, I think someone is here for you."

Rushing to the door, with a coffee cup in my hand, I see Marcus and Mr. Canderfish standing next to a homeless man.

Speaking sternly for the intrusion, I speak out.

"Hi, Mr. Canderfish, what are you doing here and why would you bring a homeless man to our door?" Looking closely into the eyes of the tall, elderly man, I gasp when I realize that I am staring into the depths of a mirror of my own eyes.

"Oh my God, Dad, is that you?"

"Hi, Rina, I would recognize you anywhere," and he steps forward and puts his arms around me.

Hearing the loud raucous at the front door, Susannah walks out with the baby in her arms, followed by Scott and Randall wearing T-shirts and pajama bottoms, and witness me being held in the arms of a stranger.

Not wanting to let go, I hear Susannah's voice, "What are you doing, Rina? What is going on? Who is this stranger?" Finally, I let go and turn to face my siblings.

"Susannah, Scott, and Randall, please meet your father."

In shock, it looks as though Susannah will drop the baby, so Alex takes baby Frankie from her arms for safe-keeping. All of them continue to stare at this stranger who resembles a much older version of our father, frozen in their steps and thoughts. Which is unusual for this family.

Frank, with tears in his eyes, tries to pull all of us into a group hug, but the three of them resist. Their anger is evident. I am ashamed of their response. When I was little, all I asked from anyone who would listen, is to let me see him again. Could he hold me just one more time? My wish has come true, so how could my siblings not welcome him back?

Aware of the tension at the door, Marcus speaks up, "I am so sorry to intrude on your Sunday morning. I wish I could help you through this shock, but your father insisted that he be brought to your home immediately. Mr. Canderfish and a good friend of mine had found your father and arranged for Frank to be picked up at the train station. Aware of my relationship with Rina, Mr. Canderfish brought him to my house and asked me to come along for support." Marcus stops talking when he sees a tall, young man walk up to Rina and pull her into his arms, then kiss her forehead.

Brandon reaches out to shake Marcus' hand, "Hi, I am Brandon, Rina's boyfriend." Marcus reaches for his hand and suddenly freezes.

Marcus does a double-take look at Brandon and speaks much too loudly. "Brandon, what are you doing here?"

Brandon looks at Marcus with a stunned look on his face and says, "Well, Marcus I can ask you the same question?" Now everyone has a confused look on their face, and we are all waiting to hear some answers.

Ignoring everyone but Marcus, Brandon asks Marcus to explain his reason for being at Susannah's home. But, before Marcus can speak a word, Rina demands to know how Marcus and Brandon know each other.

Marcus speaks first and holds up his hand to Brandon and looks directly at Rina and says, "Rina, it is a long story, but to put it bluntly, Brandon has lived with my parents since he was 12. My mother's sister and her husband died in a car accident and my mom took Brandon in. He is my cousin."

"But Marcus, you told me you were an only child and Brandon, why didn't I ever know about your cousin or that his mom and dad brought you up? You never talked about your family. I know your mom and dad died when you were young, so I assumed you were brought up by foster parents and didn't want to talk about your experience."

Marcus speaks first, "Rina, I am an only child, and I don't consider Brandon my brother. In fact, we never got along. He was a computer geek, and I was a jock. He went to college in New York, and I stayed in Los Angeles. We haven't spoken in years. Isn't that right Brandon?"

Looking at Rina, Brandon explains, "Well said, Marcus. The truth is my cousin, and I never liked each other, and it was best not to ever mention that I lived with Marcus' family. My life has nothing to do with that family and that is why I never mentioned them." And then looking straight at Marcus with venom shooting from his eyes, "But it still doesn't explain why you are at this house with Rina's father."

Stumbling over his words, Marcus says, "Rina and I are friends. We met this past summer during the filming of a reality television show. I have been working with Mr. Canderfish to help the family find their father before their mother dies."

Recognition of Marcus' explanation comes across Brandon's face, "Oh yes, she has mentioned the show to me. But it doesn't explain why you got involved in finding Rina's father. Now it is my turn to ask you to leave, Marcus."

Remembering his manners, Brandon steps forward and shakes Mr. Canderfish's hand. "Mr. Canderfish thank you for your efforts today. I think once the family gets over their initial shock, Mr. Spencer will be welcome in our home. Rina and I have this under control for now, and I think it would be a good idea for you both to leave us now."

Once the door is shut, we all usher Frank into the kitchen, with Grenada, Chuck, and Alex joining in. We sit around the kitchen table, waiting to hear what our father has to say.

After introductions, slowly, but with sincerity, Frank tells us that none of this was supposed to happen. We were meant to be one big family forever. Asking us if we knew the entire story, we all nod yes. He continues to tell us that he never wanted to leave us, but when the opportunity came, he knew that it was the only way out.

"I am not asking for your forgiveness, that is something I don't deserve. But what I am asking for is the chance to be a part of your life but in a limited way only. When your mother and I have our annual rendezvous, she has always filled me in on each and every one of you. I am so proud of what you each have become, but I am not sure if I will ever be free from the Conicci family, and I would never want to bring danger to any of you."

"When I read the message in the ad, with the contact information and Susannah's address, I knew the news would not be good. Not knowing what to think, at first, I only thought about myself. I was heartbroken. But, when I contacted Mr. Canderfish, and he shared with me the details of your mother's illness, my worst fears were confirmed. And I realized that all of you deserve my support as much as I need yours."

I can tell by the body language of my siblings, that they want to forgive Frank and welcome him with open arms. They just need time. I too find it difficult to forgive my father, but I am so happy that he is here to say goodbye to Rose.

"Frank," Susannah mutters, as the tears fall down her cheeks, "Let's put our own feelings aside for now, and I think it's time for you to see Rose. We don't want to keep you from her any longer. She has been asking for you these last few days." She stands up and reaches out her hand.

Leading him back to Rose's bedroom, Frank's steps are slow and hesitant. Susannah opens the bedroom door and waves her hand for him to go in and then she shuts the door. Not knowing what to expect, we allow him this private moment. Now that we know that their love has never died, this must be very difficult for him.

After a half hour has passed, and still the bedroom door remains closed, we become anxious. Huddled together in the kitchen, we are speechless as each of us is trying to absorb the enormity of this entire situation. Childhood thoughts are flying through my head, filled with emotion and despair. And I am sure that my siblings are experiencing the same thoughts. It is times like this, that family matters the most, and we are no exception.

Lost in our own memories, it takes several seconds before we notice our father's huge form overshadowing the kitchen doorway. The look on his face says it all. He is drowning in his own sadness, just like us.

Walking over to the cradle, he reaches down to touch the tiny fingers of baby Frankie.

"May I?" he asks, looking straight at Alex and Susannah.

"Of course," Alex states. "Her name is Frankie Rose, named after you and Rose."

The smile on his face is slight and barely reaching his eyes, but at least we notice it, as he cradles the baby in his enormous arms. It is obvious Frank is trying to control his emotions, and the baby seems to have a calming effect. After several silent moments, he begins to tell us a story. We all sit down around the massive island and quietly listen.

"Once upon a time, there was a beautiful princess who came across a very ugly toad. But, when that princess believed in that toad, they fell madly in love. That is the way I have always felt about your mother. She saved me from myself, and I thank her every day. The day each of you was born brought me so much joy."

"I never would have agreed to walk away from all of you unless I knew I had to. I will never forgive myself for that sacrifice and that is why I cannot ask you to forgive me. But the fact that your mother is suffering from lung cancer caused by the September 11 disaster is more than unforgivable. And, believe me, if there was any way I could have protected her and kept her safe, I would have. But I had to make it appear that I had died that day. I am so sorry."

And my big, strong father finally breaks down with the sobs of a giant. Although our father has aged, since last we saw him, he still gives us the appearance of a strong warrior. But the weary lines on his face, show the grief which he has had to bear, giving up his lifelong dream as a fireman, a father, and even a husband.

Throughout the remainder of the week, as we all tiptoe quietly around the house, it is obvious that our family will never be the same again. Alex convinces Frank to stay at their home for as long as he wants, and he insists on staying by Rose's bedside, and we all agree to do the same, knowing how close her time is. Rose has not spoken a word for the last five days, but we all want to believe she is aware that we are all together, once again.

Frank cannot keep his eyes off of Rose's face, not wanting to miss any sign of recognition, as he continually strokes her hand, then her cheek. He tells us about his life as a traveling salesman and some of the adventures he and Mom have been on. One of the stories surprises us when he asks us if we know that our mom is a great fisherman. I had no idea, and it makes me sad that an important part of her life had to be kept from us.

It amazes me that she led a secret life and was unable to share it with us. But, when he talks about memories of our childhood before he left, his eyes light up, he sits much taller, and we can see the love he has for us bursting its way out.

He admits that he is not sure he has the strength to live his life the way it is, without Rose giving him the strength to carry on. We tell him that although we cannot fill that void, he now has us. Today is a turning point for all of us, and I am thankful that Frank is here.

No surprise to any of us, my mom passed away in the night surrounded by her family, including our father.

As promised, she died peacefully, and she did not suffer. Last week's joy of seeing our father is now replaced with sorrow. I don't think any one of us would have forgiven our father if he didn't come home before our mother died. So much to forgive, so much to forget.

Thankfully, all the arrangements for the funeral had been made in advance, which makes it easier on all of us and allows for each of us to grieve in our own time.

Brandon's support is unexpected and now I can't stop looking at him in a different way. How could he keep such an important part of his childhood from me? I knew his parents died when he was young, but I wished he loved me enough to share his childhood experiences.

"Rina, I am unable to read your mind. Please talk to me and let me know what I can do to ease this pain. I can't imagine what you are going through. You are so strong. You always stand up for what is right and good in this world. And, for you to lose your mother, and at the same time find your father, it is mind-blowing and earth-shattering. And I am glad that Frank is here. Hopefully, all of us can draw strength from each other to deal with this loss."

"I am confused about your connection to Marcus but for now just hold me whenever you can, that is all I ask." And that is exactly what he does and why I love him so much.

Chapter 22

Marcus, 27, Former Law Student

I am not sure why I insisted on going with Mr. Canderfish to bring Frank Spencer to Susannah's home, but it was definitely a very awkward moment indeed. I feel like an idiot witnessing the astounded reactions of Rina and her sister and brothers. It should have been a private moment, and it wasn't. And, to make matters worse, I actually got to meet Rina's boyfriend, Brandon, who turns out to be my cousin. Awkward again. My intent is to provide support, but I keep forgetting I am only an outsider, not a family member like he is.

Rina texted me today to let me know that her mother passed away last night. I asked her for the details of the funeral and if she wouldn't mind if I paid my respects. She agreed that she would like that very much. It annoys me that I feel so helpless and unable to give her any type of emotional support.

Walking into the church, I immediately see Rina standing with her sister Susannah and husband. Alex. I walk over to them and give Rina a brief hug.

"Rina, I am so sorry for your loss."

"Thank you, Marcus. You remember my sister, Susannah and this is her husband Alex."

"Yes, of course. Nice to see you again, Alex. I am so sorry for the loss of your mother, Susannah. Your mother made a great impression on me when she was ordering me around when Rina hurt her ankle and cut her head. I know she will be missed."

Susannah smiles, "Thank you so much for the kind words about my mother. She was a great woman, even more so that we know more about what she has had to keep from us. Rina told me how you helped with the search for our father, and I wanted to thank you for your support."

"My pleasure, I will always be a good friend to your sister and if she is ever in need of any legal help or any other kind of rescuing, whatsoever, I am the man for her."

The stunned look and raised eyebrows on Susannah's and Rina's face make me smile. I don't think they realize exactly what I am alluding to, but perhaps I am wrong about that.

After paying my respects, I start to head out the door when a strong arm holds me back. Looking up into the angry eyes of Brandon, he whispers to me. "Stay away from Rina and her family. They do not need the likes of you hanging around. They have enough grief and sadness to last a lifetime, and you are not welcome to be a part of it." There was nothing I could do but walk out the door.

Chapter 23

Rina Spencer, 27, Freelance Writer

The house is so quiet, you can hear the sad sighs of the occupants inside trying not to interrupt the solitude of others. Every once in a while, we hear the faint sounds of baby Frankie Rose, demanding mealtime or that her diaper be changed, a lovely sound to invade the emptiness inside all of our hearts.

Scott, Randall, Chuck, and Grenada flew home today so all that remains on the hearth are me, Brandon, Frank, Susannah, and Alex as we try to pick up the pieces of our lives. Brandon is leaving tomorrow, so this home is going to feel lonelier than ever for me. And this new information that Brandon and Marcus are related has me on edge. I have this undeniably physical attraction to two men who are cousins, and more importantly, what am I going to do about it?

Even though I know it is time for me to go home, the fact remains that my father is still here and to make matters worse, I still have unfinished business with Marcus. I have to accept that it is not the time for me to leave just yet. And, besides, I want to stay and make sure that Susannah and the baby are settled in. Rose's death has created a closer bond between my sister and me, more than I thought even possible.

Brandon and I decide to go out for dinner on our last night together, just the two of us. Lately, none of us has wanted to leave the house. It has been therapeutic for all of us to be together, especially spending time with our father, Frank. Susannah, Scott, Randall, and I have not totally forgiven Frank for abandoning us, but we have all come to an understanding and agreement that family is important and Frank will always be welcome in all our homes.

His presence has us all on edge, and most of the time, he feels like a stranger to us. We are nervous that the Conicci family might find him and disrupt our reunion. We all wonder if we are in danger the longer stays he with us. Putting this stress, on top of the fact that our entire family is grieving for the loss of our mom, has not been easy for any of us.

Sitting side by side inside a booth in the restaurant with Brandon, I am feeling a little annoyed. And I start fidgeting. The noise level seems louder than usual, probably due to our quiet living circumstances of late.

Sensing my discomfort, Brandon whispers into my ear, "Would you like to go someplace else quieter?"

Trying to smile, I let him know that although the sound of people laughing, talking, and enjoying themselves is normal, I am not feeling very normal these days.

"I miss my mom so much. I don't think I will ever feel the same about anything. There is an emptiness as large as the Pacific Ocean in my heart. I want to be happy again. As soon as I see that Susannah and the baby are fine, I will come home. We, as a couple, need to spend time together. I miss 'us' and 'Brina'. I understand that your medical residency takes precedence right now, but we do need to work on our relationship. I shouldn't be having these feelings of loneliness even when we are together, Brandon, but I have."

Grabbing my hand in his, Brandon shakes his head up and down. "Rina, I agree that we need to spend more quality time together. When you return home, I promise to remind you how much I love you every day. Your mother's death and your father's return have made us all look at our lives differently."

"It makes us put the important things first and realize that nothing matters more than each other. I know you may never overcome the loss of your mother, but please know that I promise to cherish you until the day I die. I will always be here for you, to hold you, love you, and help you remain strong during the rough patches."

Tears falling slowly down my cheeks, without the energy or desire to wipe them away, I hold on to Brandon's hand with all my strength.

Fast forward two weeks. Susannah and the baby have gotten into a comfortable routine, and with the help of Mary, it is obvious I am not needed anymore. It is time to go back to New York to live the life I always planned on living. My father Frank stayed with us for a week and was very helpful with baby Frankie.

I will value those moments that Susannah and I spent with Frank in the evenings trying to understand the man he has become. Although it has been a difficult task, he began to melt down those embittered walls we built up when we found out he was still alive. When it was time for him to leave, I could tell that Susannah and I have forgiven him just a little for abandoning us. For all of us, our relationships with Frank are going to need some time.

It is not every day that you find out that the death of your father never happened in the way you thought it did. When Frank stood on the doorstep, at first, I wanted to forgive and forget, but it wasn't as easy as I anticipated. Listening to Frank tell us how difficult it was to make that choice on that fateful day of September 11, we know it wasn't easy for him either.

All these years, he loved our mother, and it amazes me that he never fell in love with anyone else. When we ask him why, all he could tell us is that he loved our mother so much, and there was no room in his heart for anybody else. He also admits that starting another family is ridiculous since he already had a family. Although we give him our permission to find another soulmate, he tells us that there is such a void in his heart since the death of our mother; meeting someone is furthest from his mind.

The three of us cry when it is time to say goodbye, but at least Frank promises that he will keep in touch with all of us on a more frequent basis. Of course, he is still paranoid about the Conicci family, so we agreed to a coded message in the *New York Times*. The next day, both Susannah and I immediately signed up for a subscription to the newspaper.

Marcus remains on my mind, but I have not had an opportunity to see him in person. Although Marcus consistently texts me with words of comfort, such as 'thinking of you'; 'when there are no words to say, just know that I am always here for you'; 'one day, he will give us the answers to questions that plague our mind'; 'time does not heal all wounds; it makes coping with the loss easier, but the heart never fully recovers'; 'death leaves a heartache no one can heal, love leaves a memory no one can steal'; or 'hold tight to memories for comfort, lean on your friends for strength, and always remember how much you are loved'. I haven't responded back to him, and I am thankful he is giving me the time I need to grieve in my own time, with my family by my side.

But I know that it is time to say goodbye to Marcus. He is not my bachelor. Nor is he my boyfriend. Nor do I love him the way I do Brandon. I have procrastinated in making this final choice, but it is the right choice.

Picking up my cell, I make the dreaded call. Thankfully, it went to voicemail.

"Hi, Marcus, this is Rina. Is it possible to set aside some time so that we can talk? Call me back, or text me and let me know when or where. Talk soon."

Chapter 24

Marcus, 27, Former Law Student

I was so happy when I listened to the phone message from Rina knowing how important it is to allow someone time to grieve in their own time. I immediately text her back letting her know that I would love to meet for dinner tomorrow night, and she agrees.

Anxious for the evening to get here, my caseload at work, is suffering. My mind keeps wandering, and I find it difficult to concentrate. I have no idea what to expect tonight. And, if she tells me she is moving back to New York, I will do anything in my power to dissuade her. What if she chooses to stay here and work on our relationship? I would be thrilled, but surprised.

The truth is, she has a life and career back in New York and a live-in boyfriend who happens to be my cousin. The obvious choice would be for her to return to New York, but one thing I am sure of, Rina is not predictable. She's stubborn, funny, proud, and definitely very independent. No one, not even me, is going to tell her what she should do. It's her choice, and that is what scares me more. I am not sure if any amount of my convincing can change the mind of someone determined to make their own choices.

Exhausted by the slow ticking of the clock, seven o'clock finally makes an appearance, and I race out of the office, eager for the union. Leaving my car at the valet, I walk in, and I am surprised to see Rina already seated at a table in the corner of the restaurant. I asked her to choose her favorite restaurant, and she told me that she had just the perfect restaurant in mind. Watching closely, without her seeing me, it is obvious why Mexican food is her favorite.

She excitedly dips a tortilla chip into the bowl of salsa and brings it to her mouth. The look that crosses her face is one of pure bliss. That look of satisfaction is definitely a turn-on. Unfortunately, she must have sensed a pair of eyes on her, so she stops what she is doing and looks up, and when she sees me, she acts embarrassed.

With a look of guilt upon her beautiful face, she states, "I thought I could wait until you got here before I delved into the chips and salsa, but they looked too tempting."

"I noticed, but don't stop on my account, it was a pleasure watching you from afar."

She laughs, grabs another chip; repeats the dipping action, and pops it into her mouth. Again, her laughter and the ease and comfort level that we have with one another always surprise me. There are no awkward moments or shyness as we talk about our activities of the past two weeks.

My past few weeks, compared to what Rina has had to endure, are definitely not as newsworthy.

"Baby Frankie is getting bigger every day. She goes to bed at 11:00 pm and sleeps until 6:00 am. That is actually good for a baby her age. Susannah has everything under control, as expected. My father decided to stay an extra week, and he was able to open up about his life. I still find it difficult to believe that he is really alive. But at least he doesn't feel so estranged as he did when he first walked through Susannah's door. He promised to keep in touch although saying goodbye was a tearful moment for all of us. And I never got to thank you for your help in finding my father. I am truly grateful." And then very quickly changes the subject.

She stops, pushes the menu to the corner of the table, and tells me she already knows what to order. This announcement amuses me. She definitely is a woman who knows what she wants.

"I love enchiladas, loaded with melted cheese inside with lots of enchilada sauce poured on top. Don't really care for the rice, but refried beans are a must. What about you, Marcus, what is your favorite Mexican dish?"

"Well, let's just say that I like all Mexican food, but the way you described the enchiladas, I am going to put my money on those."

Laughing, we both agree that a Cadillac margarita will go nicely with our choices. After we ordered, Rina gets quiet and takes a deep breath.

"Good, now that those important details are out of the way, I think we should talk about what I came here to talk about."

"OK, and what did you come here to talk about, Rina?"

"Hmmm... I think I am stalling because this is not easy for me. Maybe, I should wait for that margarita to give me courage. No, I can do this. OK, first of all, you know I like you Marcus that should be obvious. Secondly, when I think of you, I become confused, and I know why."

"I am transposing my loneliness for Brandon onto you. The fact that you two are related makes all of this easier to understand. My attraction to you makes sense. You came into my life during a delicate time for me. I live with someone, but as you know, relationships need constant nurturing."

"And although Brandon and I love each other, we have not given our relationship much time or worth since he started his surgical residency. When I came to California, I was feeling that void. I met you, and we clicked. We became friends and confidantes, and I thoroughly enjoyed our talks. But that doesn't give me the right to allow you into my heart. I want to remain friends, but we cannot be anything else."

After allowing her to speak her mind, it is my turn. "Rina, I hear what you are saying, but it doesn't mean I have to agree. I know you are in a committed relationship with Brandon, and I still can't believe that your Brandon is my cousin which makes it even more awkward for both of us. Even more confusing to me is that Brandon and I are so opposite, but you still are attracted to both of us. But I also do not want to be that person who breaks up a stable relationship, unless the person on the receiving end, meaning you, is ready to move on."

"I won't stand in your way, but I also don't want you to make the biggest mistake in your life. We have so much in common. You said, 'We clicked', and that doesn't happen often, at least for me. Your decision is complicated. You know what you have with Brandon, but are you willing to take a chance on the unknown with me? It is safe to stay with Brandon, and our connection scares you. But those are your choices, and I will honor what you decide. It's not that I am not fighting for you, because I am. But I also don't want you to be with Brandon, that is obvious."

I can tell she is hearing what I am saying, but I cannot tell if she understands completely. Her eyes are glazed over which indicates to me a sense of defeat.

Finally, there is a reprieve from this conversation when the waitress drops off our margaritas. Avoiding eye contact with me for the first time since we started this conversation, Rina takes a huge gulp of hers and sighs.

"Mmmm, good. You should try yours." When I didn't respond to her request, she raises her eyebrows and asks me if we could take a breather from the conversation. Allowing her this time, I take a sip of the margarita to appease her guilt.

Shortly thereafter, our plates arrive, steaming and delicious smelling. Again, I can't keep my eyes off her as she dives into the enchilada, savoring every bite. After she finishes all the food on her plate, she smiles and asks me if I enjoyed mine as much as she enjoyed hers. I look down at my plate and realize that there is not a morsel left on my plate. I shake my head yes although I don't remember eating the food at all. And then she starts up again.

I hold my hand up as if to stop the words that are forth-coming, but that was not my intention. "Rina, before we start back up with this conversation that I don't want to have, can you do a favor for me? And this is probably as important as the next conversation. I wrote a letter to my cousin Brandon and I would like you to deliver it to him when you go back to New York. I played a lot of unforgivable tricks on Brandon when he first came to live with us after his parents died, and I am definitely ashamed of my behavior back then. I understand why he wants nothing to do with my family, but I do want to apologize to him, not because of your relationship with him, but because we are cousins. And cousins and family should stick together; we only have each other because my parents don't count."

I hand the sealed letter to Rina, and she puts it in her purse. "Yes, I will give it to him, but knowing Brandon there is no guarantee he will read it. He has never shared any of his childhood with me after his parents died, and although I don't understand what happened between you and him, it's not my place to judge."

"Thank you." And then she goes right into it.

"Marcus, I know you are a sincere, trustworthy, and loyal man. I admire those traits. I knew tonight would be difficult, and I came here tonight with my mind already made up. Although you gave me some solid points to ponder, I think you know what I am going to say. I have to go back to New York, I owe it to myself and to Brandon. I cannot give up on that relationship so easily. I will do everything in my power to make it work, and in order to do that, I have to say goodbye to you. I hope we can remain friends, but I understand if that is not possible."

I am not surprised, but I am definitely disappointed. "Rina, like I said before, the decision is yours to make. Just remember though, if for any reason you feel like you made the wrong choice, please don't hesitate to let me know.

It's not that I will be waiting for you, but if my situation finds me available, and you want to try this relationship thing with me, I would be a willing participant. Our friendship is one I will always cherish because I care for you, and no matter the time or the distance, that will not change."

Tears are beginning to form in Rina's eyes, so she excuses herself. I watch her walk away, not sure if she will return or make a quick exit. I know she heard what I said, and I am sad about what could have been. But, from the beginning, I knew she was not available and perhaps, that is one of the reasons I want her so badly.

I finish paying the bill and wait to see if she returns. When she walks back up to the table, she smiles, pulls me up by the hand, and asks me to walk her to her car. I am glad that she made the choice to come back to the table. Walking out without saying goodbye after we just had such a serious conversation is something only a rude person would do, and she is not that type.

The valet brings her car around. I turn her toward me and plant a soft kiss on her lips. "Don't be a stranger. Please keep me posted on your exciting life. Take care, my beautiful southern belle."

She gets into the car, rolls down the window, and tells me that she will miss me.

When she pulls away, I whisper the words, "I love you and will miss you, too," not sure if she heard me or not.

Chapter 25

Rina Spencer, 27, Freelance Writer

I thought saying goodbye to Marcus was difficult; but saying goodbye to my sister and the baby was much worse. While I am packing my clothes later that night, I can't stop the tears from falling. I am supposed to be happy that I am going back to my life, and my boyfriend, but I have been here for so long, I feel like this is my home. When my mother was alive, the three of us had this wonderful chance to reconnect. We played games, retold childhood stories, and it was like nothing had changed between us.

But it did. My mom is dead, Susannah has a life with her husband and new baby, and I have to go back to New York and find out what and who I want to be for the rest of my life. I am not going to settle for less. I need to find out if Brandon is the one I want next to me each morning when I wake up. If not, then I need to make a big decision and see what there is between Marcus and myself. But, for now, one step at a time.

***

Walking around my apartment, I feel like a total stranger. I know it has been several months, but Brandon and I have lived here for two wonderful years. The walls look even more bare than I remember. The shabby couch seems shabbier. The kitchen is so tiny. I feel different and the apartment feels like a stranger. I guess I shouldn't be surprised since I have been living for the past several months in such luxury. But enough of my criticism. I must keep an open mind. I am excited to see Brandon tonight. He promised to make it an early night so that we can celebrate my homecoming. In the meantime, I will unpack and refamiliarize myself with our apartment.

For some reason, I am nervous about seeing Brandon. Although I just saw him less than three weeks ago, I can barely remember his visit. My life has moved in a fog since my mother's death. Honestly, I shouldn't be surprised by this anxiety. And perhaps the other reason for this uneasiness is the fact that I recently had dinner with Marcus and my guilt is getting the best of me. But I need to shake these thoughts of Marcus far from my mind if I want to give my relationship with Brandon a fair chance.

I can smell Brandon before he even opens the door, his arms are filled with paper bags loaded with our favorite Chinese food; Kung Pao Chicken, Moo Shu Pork, shrimp spring rolls, fried rice, and wonton soup.

"Honey, I am home."

The anxiety of seeing Brandon again is overshadowed by the mouth-watering food before me. Instantly seeing me standing by the door, he drops the bags on the counter and grabs me for a long delicious kiss which makes me forget about the food sitting next to me. Of course, the aroma of the food finally pulls us apart, and we both scramble for the bags.

The comfortable ease of our interaction with each other is a constant. Non-stop talking and eating, sharing tidbit stories about what we both have been up to since we last saw each other seems so natural. Every once in a while, Brandon reaches over and kisses me on the lips, just to let me know that he is happy I am home.

Barely able to move after eating all the food, Brandon and I clean up the mess and decide to watch the news before heading to bed. The usual news about car thefts, car chases, and local murders sounds so depressing, but when a headliner on the screen pops up about "Love at First Sight," it has my full attention. It states that there is some shocking news about the reality show that has come to light. Of course, we have to wait for the commercial break before we can hear more about it which always annoys me.

"Brandon, I can't imagine what they are going to say."

"Oh, come on, Rina. Don't tell me you are still interested in that show, are you?"

"Of course, I am. It is not every day that a person has the chance to be so close to the shooting of a reality show. Susannah and I religiously watched the show every week once we found out. And, besides, your own cousin is one of the Bachelors."

Stroking one of my hands gently, "Please can we not bring Marcus into our lives." For some reason, this request sets me off, and I pull away my hand. Brandon looks at me oddly and asks, "Why did you pull your hand away?"

"I don't want you to be upset if I should mention your cousin's name in an innocent conversation. He is a friend of mine and nothing more. I had no idea you two are related, and I don't want to feel awkward when I mention his name."

Just about the time, Brandon is going to respond to what I said, we overhear a newsflash.

Word for word verbatim from the newscaster, "Love at First Sight ratings are a farce. A source has come forward with information stating that the love-match reality show's ratings are rigged and that the producers of the show actually pay the participants to stay together."

Hearing those words, I jump up from the couch, filled with fear.

"What's wrong, Rina?"

Speechless, I don't know what to think. "Oh no, I submitted an article stating those exact words, but I asked my editor not to publish it. Do you think that they went ahead with the publication without my permission?"

"Does it really matter? The truth needed to be said."

"No, I agree that the truth needs to come out, but it was the devious way I got the information. I promised someone that I would not publish the article. How can *Lifestyles* do this without my knowledge?"

"Rina, you don't know that they did yet. Wait until the morning and when you go into the office you can find out what happened."

When my phone starts to ring, I try to ignore it. Annoyed by the ringing, Brandon asks me to answer the phone.

"No, it's not important. They can wait until the morning."

"Who are they?" Brandon asks.

Stunned and confused by all that is happening, I look at him in a daze.

Again, this time more forcefully, "Rina, who is calling you?"

"Probably, Marcus."

"Why is Marcus calling you?"

I am falling deeper into a hole with no way out. I know Brandon deserves some answers but right now, I don't know what to say without him getting further upset. But he deserves the truth, too.

"Alright, Brandon. Marcus and I are not just friends; we became close friends; and he is the one who accidentally spilled that information to me. He asked me to not divulge the information because he signed a confidentiality contract and if this information got out because of what he told me, he could be in deep shit, OK?"

Brandon continues to look at me as if he doesn't know who I am.

"Brandon, it's no big deal. Marcus and I are just friends."

"But you gave him your cell number. Are you and he going to keep in contact?"

"Yes, Brandon, that is what friends do. Don't judge me and don't blow this out of proportion, especially not tonight. Our first night together in our own apartment. I am sorry that this news ruined our plans. I will deal with everything tomorrow, but for now, can we just pretend all this never happened? I can. Can you?"

"Sure, I will try."

"Good, now I asked you not to judge me, and I will always do the same for you, but before I left California, Marcus asked me to give you a letter that he has written to you. I know your stubborn ways, and I am asking you to do a favor for me." Handing the letter to him, I finish with, "Read it on your own time, but at least read it, please."

He looks down at the letter, barely holding it as if it is on fire, and throws it on top of the mail pile. "I will when I get around to it." And that is all he said. He then takes my hand and leads me back to our bedroom.

After our lovemaking, if that is what you want to call it, I lie next to Brandon wide awake listening to his soft snoring. I am so disappointed that our reunion was nothing that I had hoped for. It was more like he was going through the motions; his heart was not in it. I feel used and abused, and I am very mad. How can he treat me like this when I was looking forward to tonight?

I can't believe his childish reaction when he found out that Marcus has my cell number. It sounds so archaic. I am not his property, and I can give my number to any person that I want to. It is the twenty-first century, and he doesn't own me. So not only do I have to deal with Brandon's stupid behavior, but I also have to find out how the story about "Love at First Sight" came out.

Finally falling asleep, I wake up the next morning totally mad at myself. Maybe I overreacted over Brandon's response to my giving Marcus my number. And the fact that I had a dream about Marcus has me feeling guilty. I can't believe that I am thinking of Marcus at a time like this. Of course, the news about "Love at First Sight" definitely bolted me out of my seat last night, but the fact that I have no idea who leaked the information has put my nerves on high alert.

Glancing at my cell phone and trying to ignore the fact that Marcus has tried to call me several times and has left at least 15 messages, does not help my mood either. Before I speak to him, I need to find out more information about the leak, and for that reason, I am anxious during my drive to the office.

Driving to work has always been a hassle, but put together my lack of sleep, I am definitely frazzled by the time I find a parking spot in the tiny underground parking garage. Walking into the office, again I feel like a total stranger. A few of my co-workers are standing by the coffee machine, anxiously waiting for their morning java. I smile and join them, pretending to be interested in their conversation about the pros and cons of underground malls. And feeling perturbed once again since I have no idea why that particular topic is being discussed.

"Hi, Rina, so good to have you back. I am so sorry to hear about your mom. Would you like some coffee?" Jo from publicity asks. Jo is probably the one person I am closest to at work. We usually have lunch twice a week, and Brandon and I double date with her and her boyfriend every once in a while.

"Thanks, Jo. I definitely need the caffeine. I could not fall asleep last night after watching the news. Did any of you hear that there was a leak about the reality dating show, "Love at First Sight"?" Watching the blank reactions on each of their faces, I can see that they have no idea what I am talking about.

So, I continue fishing for information. "Well, I guess it's no big secret that their television ratings are rigged although there has never been any proof before. It just so happens that this season's show was being taped in the same neighborhood as my sister's. In fact, right next door, I happened to meet one of the eligible bachelors. Such a coincidence, don't you think?" Again, they all continue to look at me as if they could care less. After taking the coffee cup handed to me, I casually walk away wondering to myself, why don't they care?

Eagerly waiting for an opportunity to catch a moment with our senior editor, I am constantly watching her every step. When I finally see her enter her office, I jump.

Knocking and then opening the door, I can see I caught her by surprise. "Oh, Hi, Rina. We are happy to have you back. Your friendly face has been missed. I didn't get a chance to come by your desk yet. How are you doing? I know how difficult it is to lose a parent since I lost my dad just six months ago. If there is anything I can do to help, please let me know."

"Thank you, Jennifer. I am dealing with the loss of my mother the best I can. I appreciate the offer. Can I ask you a question? Did you publish the article I wrote about the dating reality show "Love at First Sight" without my permission?"

Giving me a shocked look, she states, "Of course not. You asked me not to, for good reasons, I hope."

"Well, *Lifestyles in NYC* better not be responsible for the leak that the show's ratings are staged. Did you happen to see the news last night?"

"Yes, I watched the news, but I did not hear anything about that show. I assume that the information is true, then. What was your main reason for putting a halt on that article? It was very well written."

"My source revealed that information to me accidentally and told me that these details cannot be made public since he signed a confidentiality contract. I didn't want to create any legal problems for him."

"That is what I thought. Is there anything else I can help you with?"

Confused and dazed, all I can say is, "No, I am good. Thanks." Walking out of the office, I don't know where to begin. I know I should call Marcus and explain that I am not responsible for the leak, but it's only 5:30 am in California. And, more importantly, I need to find the source who leaked this information. But where to begin?

After several dead-end phone calls, I finally am able to speak to one of the producers at CBN news channel, who is responsible for leaking the story.

"Hi, Mr. Barron. My name is Rina Spencer, and I am a writer for *Lifestyles in NYC,* and I am hoping you can provide me with some information about a news report from last night regarding the dating reality show 'Love at First Sight?'"

"What type of information are you looking for?"

"Well, is there any way you can provide me the name of the person who is responsible for the leak?"

"As you know, Ms. Spencer, sources are to remain confidential in order to provide protection, especially in these cases."

"I understand, but you see, whoever is responsible for leaking this information may be in legal trouble."

"I assure you that the information we received was not from anyone associated with the show."

"Are you sure? I just don't see how this information could be made public without the help of someone associated with the show."

"I will only say this once, so listen carefully. I guarantee that the person who revealed this information overheard a conversation between two strangers and brought it to us. Although it was hearsay at the time, we needed to make sure that this information is factual. We contacted the show directly and have complete affirmation from the producers of the show that the information we revealed is correct. That is all I can say. Does this help?"

"Yes, it does. Thank you very much for your utmost honesty, Mr. Barron. Bye."

My entire body is shaking, waiting for Marcus to answer the phone. "Well it's about time, Rina. What took you so long to get back to me?" His voice sounds angry, and it only makes my body continue to shake.

"Marcus, I know the first thing you want to do is blame me for the leak, but you have it all wrong. I spoke to my editor, and she promised me that my article had never seen the light of day. Furthermore, I was able to find out from the news station that they personally contacted the producers of "Love at First Sight," who confirmed that the success rate of the show are not as accurate as one would think. You and I are in the clear, and I don't appreciate that you chose to believe that I was responsible. Do you distrust me that much? And if that is true, we will never, ever have any type of a future."

"I am sorry, Rina. I guess my first instinct is to blame you, but I admit I was wrong. It's not that I don't trust you, it's just that I know you work for a publicity magazine, and all they want is to provide newsworthy stories and increase circulation, and this is one way to do it... leak a juicy story. I wish I didn't jump to that conclusion, but I did."

"Honestly, Marcus, I am disappointed, but more importantly, everyone was wary of the incredibly high ratings of the show, so I don't think that anyone is surprised with this outcome. Can we ever move past this, or are you going to always hold that article over my head? It's your choice. Think about it, okay? I have to get back to work and actually try to write something worth publishing so that we can increase our circulation, talk later." After hanging up, I realize how hard I was on him, but he deserves it. He needs to understand that a relationship requires trust most of all, and we aren't there yet. Not even close.

Chapter 26

Marcus, 27, Former Law Student

After hanging up with Rina, I wish I had handled the situation differently. I am angry at myself for accusing her of leaking the story, without getting the facts straight first. I should know how important it is to have all the facts in order before building a case. Why didn't I follow what I have learned for the past three years in law school instead of attacking first?

Tonight, I need some buddy time to help clear my head. After texting the fearsome five, I wait for their response. Fortunately for me, the only one available is Peter. I think to myself that Peter is probably the best choice anyway because he is the most level-headed of all of us and the one I am closest to. I have no problem opening up to him.

We decide to meet at a local college hangout bar near USC. Big mistake. The crowd is rowdy, noisy, and rude. It's hard to believe that we fit in with them so long ago. Trying to even have a conversation is impossible. We can't even hear each other's response. Poor judgment to pick this place on my part so we agree to walk down the street to one of the quieter restaurants to grab a beer. We both agree that the subdued ambiance at the restaurant suits us.

"Marcus, it sounds as though you are missing your buddies. What's up?" Peter chimes in getting straight to the point.

Sighing, I begin to spill what's on my mind. "Well, I think I may have blown it with Rina. Did you see the news the other night about the false ratings of "Love at First Sight"?"

Peter nods his head up and down.

"Well, yesterday, I accused Rina of leaking the story. You remember that several months ago I accidentally told her that the bachelors and bachelorettes would be paid if they stayed together for three months and being the exceptional eager writer of an entertainment magazine that she is, she wrote an article about the information I divulged. When I found out that she wrote this article, she promised to never have it published. But, when I heard the story on the news channel last night, I jumped to the wrong conclusion and blamed her for the leak. And, of course, now she is angry and thinks I don't trust her and called me out. And come to find out, she is not responsible for the leak at all, and now I may have ruined any chances that I may have had with her."

"Wow, dude, you are in deep shit."

"Gee, thanks, Peter. I was hoping to hear some words of wisdom coming from your mouth, not another guilt trip."

"Sorry for being so abrupt. But let me absorb what you just said, and hopefully, I can help you out of this mess."

"Maybe I should send her some flowers and say I am sorry." "No, flowers are too easy. You need to come up with something not so cliché. Why don't you fly out and knock on her door carrying an adorable puppy and ask for her forgiveness? A girl can never say no when there is a puppy involved."

"Not bad, Peter, great idea. But there is only one problem. I am not sure her boyfriend would approve."

"Aww, man, that's right. I forgot about that major obstacle." "Well, Peter, you haven't heard the worst yet. You will never guess who Rina's boyfriend is."

"What are you talking about?"

"Do you remember my dorky cousin Brandon?"

"No way, dude. That nerd? That is Rina's boyfriend? What does she see in him?"

"Hell, if I know."

Peter laughs and tells me that if Brandon is my competition, I should have no problem winning the battle and continues to give me some sound advice.

"Well, if you are going to ask forgiveness, then I think you need to go way over the top. She lives in New York and near Manhattan, right? I think theater tickets would be a grand gesture. Of course, if you send her two tickets, she just might ask your cousin to go instead of you. That would not be cool. Hmmm, this is going to take some serious thought."

When Peter mentioned over the top, I knew what I needed to do. "Wait, I think I got it. She loves *Gone with the Wind*. Maybe I can send her a signed copy of the book. That is over the top, don't you think?"

"Yes, but it could also be a bit pricey. If she is worth it, then I say do it." Peter picks up his cell phone, presses a few buttons and whistles. "Like I said, it can be done, but it may cost you at least a couple thousand dollars or more."

"Really? Well, what is a few dollars spent in the name of love?" And that is exactly how this stupendous plan started.

It's Saturday morning, and I wake up ready to conquer the world. I jump on the computer, make a few phone calls, and head out the door by 10:00 am.

Walking into the used bookstore, a strong mildew odor instantly wafts my senses, reminding me of the law library at LMU. When the bell from the door rings, an elderly gentleman dressed in khakis, a plaid oxford shirt, and a bowtie steps out from behind a shelf of books.

"Hi there, may I help you with anything?"

"Yes, are you Mr. Brantley? I am Marcus Granger, and we spoke this morning about a signed book by Margaret Mitchell."

"Aww, yes, *Gone with the Wind*. A classic indeed."

"May I see it please?"

I follow Mr. Brantley through several mazes of shelves filled with books of all colors, sizes, and shapes to the back of the bookstore until we reach a glass-enclosed bookshelf. He takes out a loaded key chain with at least twenty keys attached, but he finds the one he wants immediately.

"I store all my rare, exquisite books inside this glass case in order to keep them safe from dust and handprints and out of harm's way." Reaching on the top shelf he pulls out a book. "I am sure you will find this one in extraordinary condition for the age of this book."

Fumbling through the pages, I am surprised my hands are shaking. I really have no idea what to look for or to even know if it is authentic. That is when he begins to point out the key criteria to look for when trying to figure out the authenticity of a book.

"As you can see, it says New York: The Macmillan Company, 1936. First Edition, first printing, with 'Published May 1936' on the copyright page. Near fine condition, with light reading curve to spine and light wear to cloth at extremities. The front and rear inner hinges are slightly exposed. Previous owner's name on front free end paper, pages lightly thumbed. And it lacks the dust cover. A lovely copy with cloth sharp and bright, uncommon in such nice condition. And it is signed by the author."

Having no idea what he just told me I say, "OK, sounds good. How much will it cost me?" I was perturbed that he wouldn't tell me the price over the phone, so I was anxious to hear his answer.

"I will sell it to you for $2,500, no less."

"No, that won't work. I was hoping to pay about $1,000."

"Well son, you came to the wrong place. I can't sell it for less than $2,000." Now we are talking. I am sure he doesn't sell too many rare books very often, so I am hoping we can negotiate on the price.

"Mr. Brantley, I just started a low-paying job after going to college for many years. The most I can pay for this book, without tapping into my monthly rent and food bill, is $1,500. Honestly, I can barely spend that much."

"Hmm, let me think about that. This is a rare find, and it is worth so much more than what you are offering, but I can tell that you are a stand-up guy, one that can be trusted to take good care of her. Am I right? What is it you actually do for a living?"

"I just passed the bar and am working in Los Angeles for a law firm."

"Impressive young man. Now tell me, who are you trying to impress with this signed copy of *Gone with the Wind*?"

Swallowing hard in order to answer his question and touching my right ear, which has always been a silly habit of mine, I quietly answer, "A girl named Rina."

"Aha, that is what I thought. Then $1,500 it is."

Whew, I am feeling relieved. I did some research on the costs of a signed book by Margaret Mitchell, and $1,500 is a good deal. Some books are selling for up to $10,000. Walking out of the bookstore, I know that both of us are satisfied with the outcome. Although he doesn't sound as eager as I know he was, I am sure not too many people enter the store with the intention to buy.

And now it is time to lay out the plan to win Rina's heart, or at least get her to continue to have contact with me.

Chapter 27

Rina Spencer, 27, Freelance Writer

It's been a week since I have been back in New York, and yet, I still feel like a stranger at work and home. My priorities are to improve my relationship with Brandon and stop thinking about Marcus even though I am still so furious at Marcus. But the next step I need to make is to talk to my editor to see if I can change the direction of my career. I am tired of writing articles that have little value, at least to me, and after four years of doing exactly that, I need a change.

Sitting at my editor's desk once again, I can see a look of agitation on her face. She probably thinks I am going to attack her again regarding the article on "Love at First Sight".

But I can see she is pleasantly surprised when I explain my desire to change the direction of my career with the magazine.

"I need some positive changes in my life, and I would like to become an editor for the magazine which has always been my lifelong goal."

"I am happy to hear that you do have some goals, and I think becoming an editor for our magazine would definitely be something I can consider. I am near retirement, but before I leave I would be happy to train you. You have always possessed eagerness, earnestness, and the ability to conquer every project that you have been assigned. I will put in a request to have you become an assistant editor. I look forward to your bright future, Rina."

"Oh, thank you so much, Ms. Bennett. I won't let you down. Please let me know when we can get started."

Once I get back to my desk, I see a black and pink mylar balloon with the words, "Thinking of you!" attached to a small, wrapped gift box.

At first, I am excited to read those words, but then I wonder who it is from. I hope it is not Marcus because I have promised myself that in order to make my relationship with Brandon work, Marcus cannot be on my mind. But how am I supposed to do that when Marcus keeps seeping into my thoughts?

Slowly, I unwrap the gift box and once I see what is inside, I am dumbfounded!

It is a very old, and well-used novel of my favorite movie and story, *Gone with the Wind*.

Pulling out the enclosed card, I read, *"Dearest Rina, A signed copy by Margaret Mitchell. A rare gift for such a rare, southern belle. Will you forgive me now? Yours always, Marcus."* Stunned, I don't know what to think. How much does something like this cost and why would he spend so much on me? I pick up the book and open it up to see Margaret Mitchell's signature. I close my eyes and move my fingers over her signature. My body begins to shake, and I have goosebumps on my arms. This is the most beautiful gift anyone has ever given me, but I cannot accept it. It is so wrong. Why would he put me in this predicament? Carefully, I wrap the book in the tissue and place it back in the box.

After work, I rush home to make a must-needed phone call, forgetting the time zone change. I leave a message asking Marcus to call me at his earliest convenience. Hopefully, he won't call too late, because this is a conversation that I don't want Brandon to overhear.

When my phone rings, it is 10 pm my time, and knowing that Brandon should be home soon, I quickly pick up.

"Hi, Marcus, first of all, I want to thank you for sending me such a beautiful gift. And, secondly, I cannot accept it. You can't buy my love, it is not for sale."

"Hear me out, Rina. I didn't buy that book to buy your love. I did it out of the goodness of my heart. I was wrong to accuse you of leaking that information about "Love at First Sight" without checking the facts first. All I want is your forgiveness."

"You always had my forgiveness, and I can't accept your gift." "The gift comes with no obligation then. Just keep it in a safe place, and when the time is right, you can give it back to me, if you want. Deal?"

"Yes, deal. I will feel better about it under those terms. Thank you, Marcus, for understanding."

"I wish that were true, Rina. So how is life in New York treating you?"

"Life is moving forward. Of course, I miss my mom every day, and I miss my life at my sister's house, especially baby Frankie, but I have some changes to make in my life which I think will help me deal with their absence. I am going to put my writing skills aside and see if becoming an editor will appease my hungry desires to be more than I am."

"That's wonderful news. I wish you the best, even though I never read any of your articles. I have all the confidence in the world that you are an exceptional writer."

Smiling at his kind words and just about the time I am ready to respond, I hear the key in the door and realize that Brandon is home.

Quickly and guiltily, I say, "Listen, Marcus, I have got to go right now. We will talk soon. OK?" And then I hang up, hoping the guilt on my face is not apparent.

"Honey, I am home!" Brandon yells. It's a phrase he says every time he enters our apartment, and it always makes me excited to see him.

"Hi, Brandon." Running up to give him a kiss on the lips. "You will be delighted to know that I actually cooked something for dinner. I am tired of carry-out and it's about time I learn to boil more than just water."

"Great," he grimaces. "What's on the menu today?"

"Don't give me that look, young man. I am thrilled to say that we will be dining in Italy today with spaghetti Carbonara. A simple dish, using only five ingredients, spaghetti, bacon, garlic, Parmesan cheese, and eggs, and it only took me 15 minutes to make. Add a Caesar salad, garlic bread, and a glass of your favorite white wine, and voila, a meal set for a king."

"Wow, what's the occasion? I am truly humbled by your gift."

"To the man, I look forward to coming home every night. This is my way of thanking you."

"Again, I am truly honored." He picks me up and spins me around and gently placing my feet back on the floor, plants a juicy kiss on my lips. "But first let me taste this masterpiece before I praise you more, my lady."

"OK, but first let me tell you that I met with my editor boss and asked if I could change directions in my career, to one of becoming an editor, and she said yes."

"Wow, that is great, Rina. I know you will be an exceptional editor, just as you are an exceptional writer."

Jolted by his words, since they were very similar to what Marcus just said, I am hesitant in my response.

Brandon gives me a funny glance, "Hey, where did you just go, the look on your face says you were a million miles away."

Quickly, I say, "Oh, it's just that for a minute, I realized that my life is going to change, and I got a little nervous."

"There is nothing to be nervous about, Rina. You are an incredible, brilliant woman, who can conquer anything she tries." He is seated at my elegant table setting with cloth napkins and lit candles, ready to delve into my Italian creation. Taking a bite, he suddenly wrinkles his nose and says, "Maybe you cooked the spaghetti just a little too long, but I am sure you can get the hang of it one of these days." And then we both start laughing, both of us unable to stop for several minutes.

After dinner, Brandon pulls me into his arms and tells me how proud he is that at least I tried. And then he shocks me by informing me that he read the letter Marcus wrote. He reaches into the desk drawer and hands me the letter. "I would like for you to see what he wrote."

Dear Brandon,

I asked Rina to bring this letter to you, and I hope you decide to read what I have written. There are several reasons I need to apologize to you. First and foremost, I want to say I am so sorry for the loss of your parents when you were 12 years old. From my understanding, your parents were the most kind and loving parents any child could have been lucky to have, so unlike me or mine. I understand why you hightailed it out of California as soon as you graduated from high school.

My parents are notorious for making a child feel like they don't matter. And then add that negativity to the way I treated you when you moved in with my family; I would hate our guts, too. My parents are the most unloving, selfish, and self-righteous people I know, and I am their son. They are both so dysfunctional to the point that they do not know how to make a child feel wanted or loved. With that thought in mind, I want you to understand how I contributed to the unwelcome home surroundings that were created when you arrived.

My parents never told me they loved me, never told me that they were proud of me, and definitely did not make me feel that we were a close-knit loving family. I am not making up excuses for my behavior, but when you walked through our door, I immediately decided to hate you for several reasons. First of all, I was jealous because they were more concerned about your welfare than my own. You became their star pupil, and I was the class clown. You excelled in spelling bees and science projects, and I excelled in sports but was never good enough in their eyes to make much out of my athletic ability.

To me, I felt that my parents preferred you over their own child, and it hurt like hell. I felt that I no longer existed because you came into the picture. So my distorted reasons for teasing and verbally attacking you at school were my way of protecting myself from the inflicted pain caused by my own parents. They will never get a Parent-of-the-Year Award that I can promise you.

I know now that all those reasons for treating you so badly were a poor excuse to lash out my hurt feelings on you. None of it was your fault, but at the time I could not see that. I was acting like a punk, and I poured out my anger on you. We were so different, you had the brains, and I did not. But that is no excuse for my behavior.

Unfortunately for you, their praising only lasted for about four months and then you also got to be the underachieving, unsuccessful, no-good-for-nothing louse that I was. I overheard my parents in their bedroom one night asking themselves how long to continue boosting your ego. After that night, they began to treat you no better than me, showing their true colors. And I saw the look on your face when you realized that no matter what you did to impress them, you no longer could.

Do you want to know the beauty of all of this? You were able to run away, start a new life, and begin again. I was very envious of your freedom to do as you pleased, with no obligation to my parents. I kept saying to myself that you were one lucky man. And here I am, still tied down to my parents who will never want to know my hopes, my dreams, my lifelong goals or even to ask how I am doing.

After years of therapy, I have come to the conclusion that I don't care what they think anymore. I go to my monthly obligatory dinners with no expectations and that is how I cope.

But look at us now, cousin? So opposite in many ways, but also driven to be the best that we can be. I am proud of OUR accomplishments... and we did it against all odds, and I am proud to be your cousin. I know that you are going to be an amazing orthopedic surgeon, and I wish you the best always.

Please forgive me for all my youthful mistakes.

Your cousin,
Marcus

After reading Marcus' letter, I begin to understand how difficult it was for Brandon's teenage years in California and why he chose not to share those times with me. There are tears in my ears when I finish reading the letter. I sit down and say, "Brandon, I never knew. I do not look at you with pity. I look at you with complete admiration and love because you overcame a very sad situation and made something of yourself any parent would be proud of." Putting my arms around his neck, I leaned in for a kiss which was very much needed.

"Although it is none of my business, do you think you can ever forgive Marcus for what he did to you when you were teenagers?"

"I don't honestly know, but at least he apologized, and I am grateful for that."

That next morning, I text Marcus and tell him that Brandon read the letter, and he is grateful for the apology. I also mention that Brandon asked me to read the letter, and I did. I tell him thank you for trying to amend the wrongs that were done to a very grief-stricken young man named Brandon.

Chapter 28

Marcus, 27, Former Law Student

Several weeks have gone by since I sent the signed book to Rina and last we spoke, and since then, there has been very minimal contact between us, except for a few texts. When she wrote that Brandon read the letter I had written and that she read it too, I am glad that at least Brandon knows how ashamed I am for how I treated him. At least some of the hurt and pain that we both have gone through can hopefully subside a little. As for Rina and what she thinks of the letter, I just hope she doesn't judge me for the behavior of a very confused, unloved, lonely teenager by the name of Marcus.

The holiday season is approaching, Thanksgiving followed by Christmas, and there is already this energetic, hustle and bustle in the air which only makes me anxious and irritated at the same time.

This distance between Rina and myself is not helping my mood, and it has me thinking that it is time to do something about it for I am fearful that the saying, 'out of sight, out of mind' might be true.

After working several long nights on case workloads that seem to be growing daily, I requested a four-day weekend over Thanksgiving and, unexpectedly but thrilled, it was granted. On Thanksgiving, I spent the day with Peter and his family since my parents never seem to include me in their holiday festivities (for which I am only thankful). My obligatory dinner with them once a month, is more than enough. Every year, Peter's mother prepares such an elaborate turkey feast. I have never turned down the offer.

After dinner, Peter and I are literally lying on their family room couch, barely able to move from all the food we ate.

"Just so you know, Peter. Tonight, I have a flight to New York to make a surprise visit to Rina."

"Dude, what are you doing? I have never seen you chase a girl, they are all always chasing you."

"That's right and look what good it has done for me so far. I can't sit back and wait for things to happen. I need to be involved, interactive, and engaged."

"Engaged? What? Are you going to propose?"

"No, bonehead, I mean engaged in the relationship, not sitting back and letting life pass me by."

"Whew, you had me worried there for a minute, Marcus. But what about Brandon, your cousin? Are you going to just show up at her home and knock on the door?"

"No, I am not an idiot. I have it all planned out. Last week she texted me that she has to work this Friday to finish up some articles. She is switching careers for the magazine and will begin her new job on December 1. So, the opportunity to show up at her office instead of her home is perfect. She also mentioned that she didn't mind working over this particular holiday since her boyfriend was going to be on-call all weekend. Bingo! Again, perfect opportunity."

"Good luck with your perfectly orchestrated plans. You do know that it may not play out the way you want, right?"

"I am keeping a positive and open mind. By the way, do you mind dropping me off at the airport? I just happened to bring my duffle with me." Watching Peter's astonished look tells me that he thinks I am nuts.

Catching a red-eye, I arrive at JFK Airport ready to conquer the day. Of course, I took an Ambien sleeping pill during the flight, which helped me to feel rested and eager for the morning to begin.

Pulling up to the glass high-rise building on 5th Avenue, which houses the offices of *Lifestyles of New York*, I am impressed with the elegance of the building along with the location, right in the heart of Manhattan. I hop out of the cab quickly. Noticing a flower stand on the corner of the street, I rush over there to purchase a bouquet of red roses. Taking a deep breath, I pull out my phone and text, *"Hi, Rina, how is your day going?"* and wait for a response.

My heart starts racing when I see the bubbles on the text line assuring me that Rina is responding to my text.

"Just wrapping up on some last-minute articles, hopefully forever. Monday, I start training to be assistant editor to my boss."

"Is it possible you may have a few minutes to talk to me?"

"Sure, what's up?"

"First of all, there is a delivery in the lobby that I have sent over. Could you please go and get it and then call me back?"

"Marcus, I don't want any more gifts from you. Remember, we talked about this before."

"Well, this is a special delivery and it's perishable. Please?"

"OK. I will call you in a few minutes."

I am anxiously hanging out in the lobby looking suspicious holding a bouquet of roses along with my leather overnight satchel. Trying to make myself as inconspicuous as possible which doesn't seem to be working with the security desk. The security officer is eyeing me suspiciously.

Finally, I hear the sound of the elevator bell and out walks Rina wearing a navy-blue flared dress that swings about her hips as she walks, her matching navy-blue pumps making tap-tap sounds on the floor. Her dark hair is pulled back in a loose-fitting ponytail, and she looks incredibly stunning. As she heads over to the security desk, I step out from behind a large planter, and she suddenly sees me. She stops dead in her tracks.

"What in the world, Marcus? What are you doing here?"

"I came to see you, Rina. Why else would I be here?" And I hand over the bouquet of flowers. "These are for the beautiful girl who always takes my breath away."

She looks up into my eyes and smiles. "You always have a way of making me smile, don't you? But what are you really doing here?"

"To see you, as I said before. I miss you, and I thought it was time I did something about it. Do you remember that time you told me that you never wanted to go to Ground Zero and see the September 11 memorial because it brought back too many memories of losing your father? You told me that you did not have the strength or the desire to go there ever. Well, I want to be the one to bring you there, and we can explore the grounds and museum together. It's time. Even though you lost your dad that day, he did not die at the Twin Towers, and now that he is still alive, it is time for you to go there, with me by your side."

"I don't know Marcus. I am still not ready. And, besides, I have to stay at work."

"Rina don't make up excuses. You just told me that you were wrapping up some loose ends. I think, if you really try, you can leave the office early today. Am I right?"

I can see she is hesitant and trying to find the right words to say no, but in reality, I can see that she is somewhat considering the offer.

Not wanting to beg, but hoping to convince her to say yes, I say one word, "Please."

Chapter 29

Rina Spencer, 27, Freelance Writer

Today was supposed to be a day filled with no pressure. I was looking forward to working at the office, with only the skeleton staff working today. I can accomplish so much more on days like these.

I have been home for several months, and I still feel like a stranger at work and at home. Brandon and I have reached a state of contentment. As a third-year orthopedic resident, Brandon's hours are so hectic. I spend many nights alone, and on these nights, I try to keep myself busy, so I don't reach out and call Marcus. He always seems to creep into my mind, and it makes me feel that I am cheating on Brandon. And, in a way, I am emotionally cheating.

And now, today of all days, Marcus shows up unannounced, looking so adorable in his acid-washed jeans and his gray wool overcoat. Pleading, with those sexy blue eyes, and exposing those adorable twin dimples, I can feel my sensibility crumbling.

"Hmmm... since you did fly all this way to see me, I think I can work something out." Glancing at my watch, "Let's see it is almost 11:00 am, why don't you go over to the Starbucks down the street, and I will meet you there in about an hour, OK? And just so you know, if for any reason I feel uncomfortable when we get close to Ground Zero, you must promise to not pressure me to stay."

"I promise, Rina. You don't have to worry about any pressures. We are just going to explore Manhattan together since I have never been here before." Grinning, he picks up his leather duffle bag.

"Marcus, would you like to leave that in my office so that you don't have to drag that around all day?"

"That would be perfect. Thanks for asking, Rina. It never entered my mind what I was going to do with it once you said yes."

Walking into Starbucks, Marcus looks so natural and relaxed sitting at one of the tables, reading the *New York Times*. The newspaper was scattered all over the table, with barely any room for his coffee drink. Sensing my presence, he looks up and tries to gather the papers to make room for me and in the process knocks his coffee cup over, spilling coffee all over the newspapers.

"Can I get you a coffee, Rina?"

Sitting down in the chair that he offers, I tell him. "I think you need one too and can you get me a double espresso?"

Raising his eyebrows in surprise, I tell him, "I think I might need the caffeine for courage." Understanding shows in his eyes.

Once he walks back with the two drinks in tow, an awkward silence happens as we both are occupied with tasting the hot liquid.

Breaking the ice, Marcus starts talking first, "Since neither of us has been to the September 11 memorial, I had plenty of time to do some research. Let's begin with a casual lunch somewhere near Ground Zero. I found this local café called, The Dead Rabbit. Sounds good doesn't it?"

Both of us begin to laugh, taking the edge off of my fear about the September 11 memorial. Smiling, I respond, "Sounds appetizing."

And that is how our day begins.

Lunch at The Dead Rabbit turns out to be more scrumptious than I anticipated. Marcus and I share a fresh burrata salad with ripened heirloom tomatoes, micro basil, and aged balsamic, along with a ham and cheese toasted sandwich. The dishes are so delicious, we don't even try to have a serious conversation. I didn't realize how hungry I was until the food was placed down in front of me.

Taking a deep breath to collect my thoughts, I begin, "In case you were wondering, I have many reasons for my reservations about going to the September 11 memorials. First of all, even though my father did not die on that tragic day, it doesn't change the fact that I thought he did. When I found out what happened to my father's squad that day and that many did not survive, my life drastically changed for the worse. September 11 molded me from that day into the person I am today. I cannot and will not forget the sadness and heartache that my family went through."

"It is not something I can just erase. And then there's the fact that my mother developed cancer from the toxic gases after looking for my father in the ashes and rubble at Ground Zero for two months. So, if you ask me, I have every right to have these negative thoughts of anything related to the Twin Towers terrorist attack. But you are right about one thing, maybe it is time to face these fears that I have harbored all these years." Standing up, I reach out my hand to Marcus and say, "Let's do it."

Walking hand-in-hand toward the September 11 memorial twin pools, which are set within the very foundations where the Twin Towers once stood, I feel a strong sense of loss and sadness. I close my eyes and pass my hands over some of the etched names of those who were killed in the attack and my body starts to shake. Opening my eyes, I try to read every name in my view: to remember them, honor them, and cry for them. Marcus, noticing my reaction, immediately stands closer to me and puts his arms around my waist, and we read the names out loud together.

And when my voice freezes, Marcus turns me around and holds me close. I refuse to quit reading the names aloud until I find the one I am looking for. And, when I find the one name I am looking for, the sobs that escape my mouth are heart-wrenching. Finally, I step away from Marcus, and with tear-filled eyes, I say, "I am ready to go to the museum now."

It is amazing that the historical exhibition museum is housed within the exact footfront of the North Tower. Our tour starts with live videos about the birth and history of the Twin Towers, then details about the days leading up to the attacks, followed by vivid videos of the planes crashing into the towers, and then the heartbreaking replays of the two Towers tumbling. Displayed throughout the museum are many of the remaining artifacts and mangled metal left over from the towers. Together, Marcus and I came to understand the heroism involved in the aftermath of first responders, emergency personnel, and the many volunteers who tried to help save as many lives as they could. But, more importantly, we are able to recognize a sense of hope that is encompassed by the beautiful acts of compassion and public service from around the country and around the world. Emotionally exhausted, we walk away, feeling at peace.

On the taxi ride back from the memorial, both of us are unusually quiet. We are sitting side by side, and Marcus is holding one of my hands. Once we reach my office, Marcus asks if I would like to get some dinner before I head home.

Initially, my first response is to say no. But then I remind myself that Marcus flew all this way to be with me. And, even though we had an amazing day together, and I am still totally drained, it won't hurt to end the evening on a more cheerful note.

Laughing out loud, I tell him, "Even though I don't feel that hungry, once I smell food, it's always the opposite. But I think I would like to go somewhere quiet, so we can just sit and enjoy each other's company, if that is alright with you?"

"That sounds perfect, and I would like to make a suggestion, and I understand if you say no."

I raise my eyebrows in question, and he continues, "My hotel room is just a block away. Once I check in, we can go up to my room and order room service which will give us the peace and quiet we crave." Smiling, he adds, "I promise to be on my best behavior."

Hesitant at first and then with more conviction, I agree with his suggestion. We pick up his duffle bag from my office and head over to his hotel. Once in the room, an uncomfortable silence overcomes us while we keep ourselves busy looking at the room service menu. We decide to order a simple selection of two hamburgers and a bottle of wine. And, then without warning, I am shocked by this strange sense of excitement, standing so close to this disturbingly, attractive and enigmatic man. My blood starts to stir every time Marcus's eyes meet mine.

Marcus steps closer to me and pushes back a strand of hair that has fallen over one of my eyes. My pulse begins to quicken, knowing full well there will be consequences to these impulsive actions that I don't want to turn away from.

Even though we have not spent much alone time together, there is no doubt that I am drawn to him. It is more than his brooding good looks, or his lean, muscular body; I feel a special connection when we are together. This is where I choose to be, to be close to him, to have him touch me, and hold me.

Still facing me, Marcus keeps his eyes on me, as mine are tracking his. He takes one step forward and brings his hand up to my cheek, and with that movement, I take a small step toward him. Unable to resist the magnetic pull that is drawing us closer to each other, he slips one arm around my waist, and effortlessly pulls our bodies together. With his other hand, he slides it beneath my hair, cradling my head, he tilts it up toward him. Our lips meet and all sensible restraint, any common sense to break it off, melts away. We stand like this for several minutes, our lips, mouths, and hands hungrily exploring.

When Marcus begins to unzip my dress, I offer to assist. Once it falls to the ground, he picks me up and carries me over to the huge king-size bed. He studies my face, his own face reflecting passionate yearning, and cautiously, leans over me, and with both hands, gingerly touches my bare, exposed skin. I close my eyes.

Since he is fully clothed, I try to undo his belt buckle, he climbs up on the bed on top of me and kisses my breasts over my pink lacy bra (thank goodness I had the sense to wear it tonight and not one of my every day flesh-toned ones). I arch my body with sensuous delight. Waiting for more, I definitely want more. I open my eyes and gaze at Marcus' face and witness a serious expression transform across his face.

Marcus pulls away and swears. "Rina, I made a promise that I will not put pressure on you to do anything you don't want to do. I am so sorry for my poor behavior. Just say the word, and I will stop right now. But, just so you know, you stir so much unbelievable passion and desire in me, I will not be able to stop if we go any further."

Now it is my turn to be in control. I am truly impressed by Marcus' concern for my reputation which not only personifies the moral character of this sexy man, but it allows me to be the one making the choice. It is obvious that this is not just a matter of simple lust. The electrical chemistry we have for each other is preciously unique.

All my life, I have never had to make difficult choices when it comes to matters of my heart, and I know that what I choose to do at this exact moment will determine my future. It seems that it would be much easier to talk myself out of this precarious predicament, knowing full well I will have some type of regret if I don't. But is it wrong to pass up this chance when moments of beauty and love are fleetingly rare?

Sensing my indecision, Marcus is impatiently waiting for some type of reaction from me. And, just like that, the magic is broken with a knock on the door.

I quickly stand up, grab my dress, and run to the bathroom. Walking out, now fully clothed, I find the words I want to say, "There is nothing to forgive, Marcus. It takes two to tangle, and I was as much of a willing participant as you. What we have is rare and beautiful, and we should not feel ashamed for this behavior. And that is what scares and excites me at the same time."

"I knew from the first time we met, that there is something amazing and undefinable between us. We cannot deny it anymore. But you are right, let's not have any regrets. Let me figure out what I want first. I know that is not fair to you, but you knew exactly what you were getting into from the beginning. Nothing has changed and then, everything has changed. Oh, my God, that food smells delicious. Can we eat now?"

Laughing at me in his stocking bare feet, with his pants now fully zipped, I can't help but laugh when he says, "That is exactly what I adore about you, Rina, a woman with an appetite."

Closely watching Marcus while he is ferociously eating his hamburger, I can see that he is trying hard to control his own emotions. I am so grateful for his moral conscience because there is no doubt in my mind that if he hadn't stopped us when he did, I would have willingly and joyfully given myself to him, my whole body and soul.

Thankful for the way the night ended, my taxi ride back to my apartment has me thinking. Walking away from Marcus tonight is one of the toughest decisions I have ever had to make. I am so torn and confused about my future. I foresee too many changes ahead, and I am not sure how I should feel about them. It also helps if I keep reminding myself that Marcus is not my bachelor, but, then again, is that true anymore?

Chapter 30

Marcus, 27, Former Law Student

After putting Rina in a taxi, I watch her drive away with mixed emotions. Sadness because I let her go, not knowing when we will see each other again. And happiness because there is actually more hope that one day she may actually choose me. We came so close to making love tonight and based on that incredible spark of passion that we experienced, I will never settle for less. Of course, I was disappointed when I asked her last night if she would meet me for an early lunch before my flight leaves tomorrow, but I understand where she is coming from.

Her plight may even be more difficult than mine is. But the decisions are all in her control. I told her that I would not wait for her forever, but if and when she makes a choice, and it is me, I will definitely be open to the idea of seeing where we go from there. And, in the meantime, I need to move on with my life. And one thing I promise myself is no more reality television shows.

The next morning, with no definite plans and plenty of time to spare before my flight, I decide to walk along 5th Avenue. Surrounded by all the shoppers bustling about, coupled with the honking, and crazy taxi drivers darting in and out of lanes, I am reminded how sedate Los Angeles is compared to Manhattan and look forward to getting home.

Walking into my empty apartment, I realize how lonely my life is without Rina. I miss her already, even though I just saw her yesterday. It is going to be difficult to not think about her, but I know that is what I must do. Unpacking and surfing the television channels for a show that catches my attention. I know I must live my own life.

The next morning, I have a difficult time waking up. It is Monday and knowing that I have the entire workweek ahead of me, my energy level is shot. Forcing myself out of bed, I hop in the shower and turn the water on cold. That does the trick, as it always does.

Sitting at my small kitchen table, coffee in hand and newspaper spread about, my phone rings.

"Hello."

"Hi, Marcus, this is Rina."

"Hi, Rina, I am glad you called. Is everything alright?"

"Yes, I just wanted to say thank you for escorting me to the September 11 memorial exhibits. Since that day, I carry around this feeling of calmness and tranquility deep inside that I have not experienced in such a long time. Ever since my mom died, I have had trouble sleeping and have not been able to shake away these nightmares about losing my father all over again. But, ever since our day together, the nightmares have disappeared, and I want to let you know that if it were not for your insistence, I might never have gone there. You brought some peace back into my life, and I am very thankful for that."

"I am happy to oblige, Rina. Please never hesitate to call me if ever you need to talk. I will always be here for you, as promised."

"Thank you, Marcus. I guess I better get back to work. Today is my first day as the new assistant-editor-in-training. Sounds impressive, doesn't it?"

Laughing out loud, I tell her, "Best title ever. Knock them dead, Rina. You got this."

After hanging up, I decide not to allow these small talks between us to give me false hope. Even though I am so happy that she calls, it doesn't make the loneliness disappear; it only makes me miss her more.

My morning schedule is nothing to brag about, and usually, an interruption can only add some thrill to it. As it goes, before I shower, I usually do 100 sit-ups, followed by 50 push-ups, and finally, I make several bare-fisted stabs at the punching bag suspended from the ceiling of my living room. It is just a mundane routine that allows me to feel better about myself the rest of the day.

Arriving at work ready to delve into my workload, I see a message on my desk that Mr. Turner, one of the partners, requests my presence in his office at 9:00 am sharp. Of course, this request has me concerned.

Walking into Mr. Turner's office, I am in awe of the simple beauty of the immense office, from the wall-to-wall deep mahogany built-in bookcases, loaded with thousands of prestigious law books, I feel dwarfed standing next to the massive mahogany desk, completely void of any files, paperwork or pens. And, behind the desk, sitting as straight as any human could possibly sit, is Mr. Turner. He points to one of the chairs facing him, and I quickly take a seat.

"Well, Marcus, I think it is time we get to know one another a little better. Please don't look so worried. I am not here to administer any criticism. You are doing a fantastic job, from what I am hearing. But, as one of the founding fathers, it is my responsibility to make everyone working for the firm know that we consider everyone one big, happy family. And, in order to do this, I like to sit down and have a little chat with the newbies."

Laughing out loud, he continues, "That is a term I can't come to terms with, but it is what everyone keeps calling all the new incomers. I hope you don't mind if I delve right in and ask you to tell me a little about your upbringing. I understand that your parents are somewhat famous in the television news business."

Clearing my throat, never expecting the conversation to go this way, I tell him the truth. "Yes, both my parents worked very hard to get where they are today. They are both very success-driven, and I am proud to be their only son."

"They must be very proud of your own success, too?"

"Well, let's just say they that their high expectations of me are being met."

"Good to hear. Now, another reason I requested your presence today is to personally invite you to my 50th wedding anniversary next Saturday. I have extended a personal invitation to everyone in the firm, and I hope that you can make it."

"I would feel honored to attend such a happy celebration."

"Great, my secretary Betty will email you the necessary information with time and place. Looking forward to seeing you there."

Riding down the elevator, I am finally able to breathe again.

Arriving at Turner's enormous Tudor style home in Westwood, I am dressed in the required black-tie attire. The home is beautiful as expected, and very merrily decorated with white Christmas lights twinkling in the trees, sidewalks, and planters. A valet takes my less-ostentatious car, and walking into the foyer, I am surrounded by other guests dressed in their gala clothes. An enormous 20-foot brightly decorated Christmas tree greets us, as we are ushered into a huge ballroom also festively decorated with white twinkling Christmas lights. Uniformed waiters and waitresses are professionally scampering around offering flutes of champagne and mounds of tiny, delicious shrimp and crab appetizers.

I take a glass of champagne although the sole reason for driving here myself is to control my alcohol intake. It has been the downfall of many employees to imbibe in too much alcohol at work-related functions, and I am not going to fall into that category. I also take a shrimp morsel and pop it into my mouth.

At about that time, Mr. Turner walks toward me with a very young beautiful dark-haired woman dressed in a daring low-cut black gown attached to his arm and begins to introduce her to me. For a second, I start to choke on the shrimp because I never expected his wife to be so young. He told me it was his 50th wedding anniversary, and I don't believe unless she has an exceptional plastic surgeon, that this woman is over 25.

Noticing my discomfort, he asks, "Marcus, are you okay?" Taking a sip of the champagne, still trying to swallow the shrimp that in its entirety is stuck in my throat, I am unable to speak but manage to shake my head up and down.

"I would like to introduce you to my daughter, Gabriel."

Coughing to clear my throat to speak, but before I can stop it, the shrimp shoots out of my mouth and lands deep in the cleavage of Gabriel's plunging neckline. Gabriel and Mr. Turner first glance down at the shrimp lodged between her breasts and then look up at my astonished, embarrassed face and start hysterically laughing.

The sounds of their loud laughter bring over a beautiful older version of Gabriel, also dressed in a stunning flowing black gown, and Mr. Turner introduces her, "And this is Sandra Turner, my beautiful bride of 50 years."

Finally finding my voice, although what I really want to do is crawl under one of the many cocktail tables, I squeak out, "So pleased to meet you both, and if you don't mind, I think I must excuse myself. I seem to have lost my manners, and I need to find a bathroom with a bathtub to drown myself."

Still laughing, Gabriel grabs my arm and says, "No you can't get away that fast Marcus the lawyer. I think you might need some more refreshments since you didn't get to taste the last one you had." And she reaches between her breasts and pulls out the measly shrimp and pops it into her mouth. Reaching for my hand, she pulls me away from her parents and that is how my night begins.

She tells me all about herself. She is currently a junior at Stanford studying Political Science, with law school as part of her future plan. She is also an only child, and it is obvious she has both her parents wrapped around her baby finger. I find her bubbly, way of talking in such a fast tempo, fascinating. She is bright and has a mind of her own. She doesn't take no for an answer, so is used to running every show she stars in.

She is sexy and sure of herself. When we dance, she makes sure to let me lead although I can tell at times she wants to take over. A few times, I had the privilege of watching her greet arriving guests, and I see the respectful admiration they give her. She enjoys playing the dutiful hostess, but she always finds her way back to me, of which I am grateful for. By the end of the night, when our eyes lock on each other across the crowded room, there is no distance between us.

When we part later that night after numerous dances and sexual eye contact, I ask for her phone number and when she says yes, I want to yell 'yippee'. But, instead, I pull her close and kiss her softly on the lips although I can tell she wants more. And I say to myself, not tonight. Tonight, I am in control.

Gabriel Turner, age 21, turns out to be an exciting young woman who knows how to have fun. With Christmas shortly approaching and the fact that she is home for the holidays, I have never embarked on so many holiday festivities in my entire life. Together, we have gone Christmas tree hunting, caroling, snowmobiling, sledding, ice skating, and more alarming to me, Christmas shopping.

Gabriel has such a big heart and is that type of girl who wants to buy a gift for everyone, no matter how small the connection. Thus, here I am walking through a very crowded mall in Costa Mesa, with my arms loaded down with packages, as Gabriel leads me into the next store.

"Gabriel, hold on a second. Can we please take a break and put these packages in the car before we pile on more packages?" Finally, she stops and actually looks at me standing there with too many packages hanging from each of my arms. And then she laughs and grabs some of the packages. That is the kind of girl she is and why hanging out with her from time to time has been loads of fun. No obligations, just plain fun.

Chapter 31

Rina Spencer, 27, Freelance Writer

It is Christmas Eve, and Brandon and I are enjoying a rare night out together at the hospital annual Christmas party. Brandon looks extremely handsome in his rental tuxedo, and I feel like a princess, in my black sequined cocktail dress. With a glass of champagne in our hands, I am introduced to many of the residents that Brandon works with. Some of them are married and others are flying solo tonight. After the introductions and we begin to walk away, one of the female residents is very obviously staring at me. I believe her name to be Rebecca, so I ask Brandon what is her story?

"Rebecca is one of those doctors who believes that no one is better than she. You know the kind, always raising her hand first to be chosen for surgery, or just always lecturing to us as though she is the expert. I find her annoying, to say the least. Why did you ask?"

"Well, when we were introduced she looked at me as though she knew me and now she can't stop staring at me."

"Why don't you go up to her and ask her why."

"I will. She just walked into the restroom, and I am going to talk to her." Handing, Brandon my empty glass of champagne, I walk toward the restroom with a purpose after finishing my glass of champagne.

Waiting impatiently, I dab some lip gloss on my lips in front of the mirror. Rebecca walks out from one of the stalls and sees me.

"Hi," she says. "Have we met before? Your name is Rina, and you are with Brandon, right? You just look so familiar to me, and I never forget a face."

"Nope, Sorry, I don't believe that I have met you before."

"I know you look familiar, and I will figure it out before the end of the night," Rebecca says as she walks out of the bathroom. I shrug my shoulders and follow her out. She whispers something to Brandon and walks away.

Surprised, I ask Brandon what did she whisper to him? "She told me that she knows my girlfriend from somewhere and that I need to protect my heart."

"What is she talking about Brandon? Why would she say that to you?"

Shaking his head, Brandon says, "I have no idea."

Now our entire festive evening has just taken a turn for the worst. Rebecca has me wondering who she is confusing me with and why would she involve Brandon into the situation.

The rest of evening, both Brandon and I try to forget about wacky Rebecca. We drink more champagne, eat a fabulous prime rib dinner and dance the night away. After the last song, both of us are looking forward to getting home and just enjoying some alone time together with no interruptions. We are standing outside in the cold air waiting for the valet to bring around our car, and I see Rebecca heading toward us. I suddenly freeze up, which gets Brandon's attention. She sashays up to both of us with a knowing grin and says out loud so everyone within close distance can overhear, "Brandon, you better be careful, I saw your girlfriend holding hands with another man walking into a hotel together."

With no hesitation, I hear Brandon stand up for me and tell Rebecca to mind her own business and quit spreading rumors about his girlfriend.

When he turns around to give me his winning grin, he sees that my face has gone entirely white and tears are welling up in my eyes. Without as much as a goodbye, I watch Brandon turn away from me and walk down the street.

Embarrassed by this entire predicament, I bravely stand and wait for the valet to pull up my car. Walking into the apartment, I am not surprised to find Brandon not at home.

When the Sunday morning sun and Christmas Day make its rude appearance through our bedroom blinds at 6:30 am, I moan and pull the bed covers over my head. An hour later, I check my phone on the nightstand, and still, there is no word from Brandon, either by text or telephone call.

I have no idea where he slept last night or if I will ever be able to explain away all that he has heard. I leave a text telling him that we need to talk and that I can explain everything.

When evening comes and still no response from Brandon, I am at a loss. Will he ever let me explain what that girl named Rebecca saw and if I do tell him, will he believe me that nothing happened because of what Brandon and I have together? I know that when I do confess what did happen that night in the hotel, I may never regain his trust again. It is like a no-win situation, and I am not sure of the outcome. I make a rash decision and decide to explain myself via a text message.

Dearest Brandon,

My heart is breaking over the fact that you have been hurt by my actions. I am so sorry you had to hear about my escapades by someone other than me. It is true that I walked into a hotel near my office with someone other than you. But if you would hear me out, I will explain the circumstances and give you a chance to absorb the information and make a choice with what you want to do.

The other day when I was working at my office, Marcus, your cousin, stopped by to see me. We are friends and friends only. He made a suggestion, which at the time made sense to me. He offered to take me to September 11 Ground Zero memorial site. At first, I said no. But after much thought and knowing that my dad did not die in the Twin Towers, I decided it was time for me to put my fears at rest, and I said yes.

I had an emotional day walking around the museum. But by the end of the day, my spirits were lifted with such an enormous sensation of peace. I faced my fears, and I survived. I cried all day, but those tears were a positive energy of release for me. And I was thankful that Marcus stood by me that day.

Later that evening, I was hungry and exhausted that I wasn't thinking clearly when Marcus offered to order room service at his hotel room to avoid the crowds. So, we did go up to his room, but I want you to know that nothing happened that I should be ashamed of.

I should have told you about that day, and that is where my fault lies. I hope you know that I never want to hurt you. I know I made a mistake, but I hope that you also know that I love you with all my heart.

Love,
Rina

Brandon's response was immediate.

Dear Rina,

Your explanation seems vague to me. You explained what you physically did, but you did not explain clearly enough what Marcus is to you. You two seem to be very close and of all the men in the world, it has to be Marcus. The one person I had hoped to avoid forever. You allowed him to take you to a place that is very personal to you. I have offered to take you there many times, and time and time again, you refused to go. That hurts more than you will ever know. You tell me that you are only friends, but I don't agree. He obviously means more to you than you think. Even though I still love you, I don't know if I can ever trust you again. I need time to think things through. I plan to stay at a friend's home for a while. Let me know when you are away from the apartment, so I can pick up some clothes.

Merry Christmas,
Brandon

    This is some Merry Christmas. Struggling with Brandon's response back to me. I make a quick decision. I decide to fly back to visit my sister and the baby. Brandon needs time, and I want to allow him his space.

Dear Brandon,
*   I hope one day you forgive me and can trust me again. No need for you to stay at a friend's home. I made airline reservations to fly back to California to visit my sister tonight. My father is in town, and I can't wait to spend time with baby Frankie. I hope we take the time to talk things out during this separation.*

Merry Christmas,
Rina

Chapter 32

Marcus, 27, Former Law Student

The holidays turn out better this year than expected. Gabriel is like a ray of sunshine that has brightened up every day since we first met. Unlike many relationships, ours is based on no obligations. If I am free and she is free, we do something about it. Of course, work takes precedence over everything, but Gabriel is very understanding. And, besides, she grew up out here and has lots of friends and family to keep her occupied.

It is Christmas Eve, and Gabriel and I decide to celebrate by making our own turkey dinner. Since neither of us has ever tempted such a feat, we both know that we will have fun trying to pretend we are real adults. Choosing the turkey turns out to be a debacle itself. How does one know what kind of turkey to buy? How much should it weigh? And should we get a frozen or uncooked one? That was our first mistake.

Not thinking straight, we overlook plain common sense and choose a 10-pound frozen one. When we get home, we realize our dumb mistake. Trying to thaw out the turkey in one hour is not easy. Once the outer part of the turkey is thawed out, we try to pull the turkey parts in the plastic bag out of the inside of the turkey which is impossible, so we decide to cook the turkey anyways. Again, big mistake. Thankfully, we decided to buy several bottles of wine when we bought the turkey.

I have not talked to Rina since Thanksgiving and our texts have been polite but vague. I sent a text to Rina this morning wishing her a Merry Christmas, but I have not received a response back.

Once dinner was over, (we ended up ordering pizza) all I want is to sit on the couch and watch football, but Gabriel has something different in mind. She suggests we call up a few of her friends and have them over for cocktails. I tell her I do not want to do that and would just enjoy the evening alone with her. Not used to hearing the word 'no', we get into an argument, and she has one of her tantrums and storms out of my apartment.

Gabriel is a handful, but I am thankful that she keeps me so busy that I don't have time to think about Rina. But, unfortunately, the more time I spend with Gabriel the more I realize how different we are. She is always on the go, with no time to relax. She always wants to meet up with friends for dinner or at their homes. She has so much energy and never tires of going out on the town.

I, for one, enjoy a quiet evening at home once in a while. Sitting by the fireplace, sipping on a glass of wine, enjoying the peacefulness of just being home. But, obviously, Gabriel thinks differently. I like being around her, she has a positive energy that lights up a room when she enters it. People are drawn to her, and it is obvious that their adoration is a key motivator to Gabriel's ability to shine.

On the personal side of our relationship, sex with Gabriel is good because she brings that same electric excitement to the bedroom. But I want more than just good sex. I want a relationship that makes me want to give that person all of me. I want a relationship that is all-consuming. One that each of us together is greater than what we have apart. I don't feel that with Gabriel. She is a star all on her own, and she knows it.

New Year's Eve is approaching, and Gabriel is in her element. She has decided to plan a huge party at her parent's home. Today, my duties are to be the chauffeur to Gabriel. Her list of things to accomplish today is overwhelming to most, and especially to me. But I have to give her credit. She sure knows how to get things done. We have personally been to individual shops and stores to order the flowers, the appetizers, the main course, and the dessert. She tells me that there is no way that one vendor can do the entire meal. Now that is a surprise to me. But Gabriel knows best.

"Marcus, turn left into the next driveway. I want to personally pick out the wines that I will be serving that night, and I have arranged for us to do a wine tasting."

Surprised at her words since I know that Gabriel does nothing in moderation and it is only 1:00 in the afternoon, I decide to voice my opinion.

"That is fine, Gabriel, but I think I will pass on the wine tasting. Drinking and driving has never been acceptable to me."

Not even waiting for me to pull into the parking spot, Gabriel opens the car door in such a rage that her purse goes flying out of the car and empties itself in the parking lot.

"Oh, just great, Marcus. Look what you did?"

"I did not throw your purse out of the car. You, in your haste, opened the car door while the car was still moving."

"Hummpf, blame it on me. That always seems to be your ammo."

"Whatever Gabriel, can we just behave like adults and go and get the wine. I am exhausted catering to your needs all day."

"You aren't doing anything but driving the car. I am making all of the decisions, and you have not helped me one bit there. The one time I ask for your input, you turn me down."

Still sitting in the car, we continue to discuss her needs and her wants, while her purse and personal items remain scattered in the parking lot. Finally, she tells me to just leave her there, and she will get a driver to pick her up when she is done. After getting out of the car, she has a few last words for me. "Don't bother coming to the party, I decided that I am going solo that night." Which is fine with me. I would rather do nothing on New Year's Eve than have to cater to her wishes any longer. It was fun while it lasted, but I am glad that it is over. Like I said she is a handful, and she is used to doing things her way. Too much drama for me.

Chapter 33

Rina Spencer, 27, Freelance Writer

Susannah and baby Frankie meet me at the door when I arrive. Susannah looks like a picture of happiness holding this pudgy, angelic baby. Frankie has doubled in size and has this huge smile on her face. We FaceTime every day from New York, and it is obvious that she recognizes me. When I put my arms around them to hug them both, my unshed tears began to shed.

Susannah's soft coaxing voice helps to soothe me. "It's going to be just fine, Rina. You have had a difficult year like most of us, but you always try to be strong. It's good to cry. Crying helps the heart heal faster."

"I haven't been able to cry since Brandon walked out, and why it decides to show its ugliness now is not the best timing." Finishing that sentence, Susannah realizes what I am referring to when baby Frankie's mouth suddenly puckers up, her eyes swell with tears, and she lets out this piercing scream and begins to cry.

Shocked by the noise level of Frankie's scream, I immediately try to soothe her. "Oh, I am sorry Frankie, Auntie Rina is not sad. I am so happy to see you." And I start kissing her rosy chubby cheeks. But Frankie will not stop crying.

Trying to soothe Frankie is making matters worse, and my sister tells me, "Don't worry, Rina, you will get used to Frankie's way of voicing her opinion."

Once I unpack and give Susannah time to calm down baby Frankie. I venture back downstairs into the kitchen, and I see my dad, Frank, attempting to feed baby Frankie. Frankie is definitely in charge. There is more green smashed food, on Frank and the high chair than going into Frankie's mouth. It is a comical site to see.

Laughing, I walk over to Frank to kiss his cheek. He is so focused on trying to feed Frankie that I startle him, and he drops the bowl of smashed green goo on my foot.

"Thanks, Dad."

Frank laughs and says, "No worries, I think sharing is a good thing. It sure is good to see you, Rina. I had hopes to drop by after the New Year to visit with you and Brandon, but this saves me a trip. You just made this holiday merrier."

I just smile and don't explain my situation. There is a time and place to talk about serious business, but it is hard to be serious when your father is sitting there with green goo hanging from the top of his head to his left ear.

Later that night, after baby Frankie is asleep. Susannah opens a bottle of chardonnay, takes two wine glasses and gestures for me to walk with her outside to my favorite spot, the gazebo. This place has given me a lot of memories, all good. The weather is a little cooler, and typical of my sister, she has two warm fuzzy blankets on the bench ready for us to snuggle in.

"Rina, tell me what is going on with you. You were brief when you told me you were flying to California. What is going on with you and Brandon?"

Not knowing where to begin, I explain what happened. Once finished, I sigh and shake my head. "I don't know what Brandon wants. I truly hurt him, and I have no idea if he can ever trust me again. I choose Brandon, but I am not sure that Brandon wants me. He believes that Marcus is more than just a friend to me."

"Is he just a friend?"

"I don't know, but I want to believe that we are just friends. Nothing happened between us but a passionate kiss, and I might have wanted more, but we didn't go there. I felt guilty after the kiss and couldn't wait to get back to Brandon. Doesn't that mean that I choose him?"

"Are you trying to convince yourself that you choose Brandon because it is the right thing to do, and you don't want to hurt him? That is not a reason to choose Brandon. You will hurt him more, and even yourself, if you stay with him for the wrong reasons. You have to look deep into your heart and ask yourself who you want to wake up every morning with. Whose car do you want to be parked next to yours in the garage every night? If you can say Brandon, then he is the one. But, if you are hesitant and not sure, then you may have more feelings for Marcus than you admit."

"Gee, Susannah, I hear what you are saying, but I am not sure that I agree. I love Brandon. I want to be with him day and night. But, when I am with Marcus, I begin to question my happiness with Brandon."

"Let me explain it this way. As humans, we are intended to be monogamous. But just because you get married or whatever living situation it is, it doesn't mean that you cannot be attracted to someone else. But the key to this dilemma, and this is where the truth lies, is whether or not you do something about that attraction. You love Brandon but are also attracted physically to Marcus. Depending on your love for Brandon and whether or not he is your soulmate; the person you can't live without; that will determine what you do with this attraction for Marcus. It's okay to be attracted to someone other than your partner, but it's up to you what comes next."

"That makes sense to me. So, what I have to figure out is, who is my soulmate? I have many years of history with Brandon and new history with Marcus. How can you measure that?"

"Rina, you can't measure love. It's not about who you knew longer. It is about who your heart feels strongest about. There are a lot of unanswered questions to think about. I am going to leave you with these thoughts, and I hope your thoughts lead you in the right direction. I love you, and I am here for you. I love you so much, now go get some sleep."

When I get back to my bedroom, I see my cell phone on the bed, and I hope for a message from Brandon. There is none. Glancing at other texts, I notice the Merry Christmas message from Marcus. I decide not to respond tonight. Tomorrow will bring brighter days and better choices for me.

The next morning, I wake up with a slight headache. I feel guilty for running away from my problems. I know I should have stayed in New York and talked to Brandon, face to face. Will he ever forgive me for all of my poor choices? I love Brandon, and I don't want to lose him, but Susannah has me thinking about what love truly is. Is it that all-consuming feeling of passion that gives a person a purpose to live? What is a soulmate and who decides when you find one?

Brandon and I have been together for many years, and I cannot measure those years to what I have with Marcus. But Marcus also gets me. He knows who I am and has no expectations from me. I don't want to feel obligated to choose between Brandon and Marcus. And nobody should expect me to. I don't know if Brandon can ever trust me again, and that is where the problem lies. He said he will always love me, but love is not blind. I hurt him, and he has every right not to forgive me.

Walking into the kitchen, Susannah is feeding baby Frankie, and my dad is reading the newspaper with a cup of coffee. Both of them look at me, waiting for me to speak.

"What? Why are you two looking at me that way?"

Susannah speaks first, "Nothing, we just hope that you understand that we are here for you whenever you want to tell us what you want to do. I know you mentioned that you have to go back to New York after the New Year's. Is there anything you want to do while you are here?"

"Thanks, Dad and Susannah. I know that you only want what is best for me. I just need time to think about my next steps. There is nowhere I want to go while I am here. But my first step is to try and reach out to Brandon, but I am not sure he will respond. If we can't talk about what happened, I don't know how he, and I can resolve anything."

Susannah hands me a cappuccino and leads me out to the gazebo. "I can't tell you what you need to do, Rina. But I can give you some sisterly advice. Don't dwell on the past, work on the future. What I am trying to say is that if Brandon truly loves you he will learn to forgive and trust you again. Right now, he's feeling hurt and abandoned. Maybe it wasn't the smartest to leave New York, but it is too late now. Call him. Give forgiveness a chance."

"You are right. I shouldn't have left last night, but I felt lost, and I needed to be here, where I feel safe and loved. I am going to call Brandon. If he doesn't answer, I will leave a message. I will beg him to call me back. I won't take no for an answer. Thank you, Susannah."

"No problem. I will leave you alone to make that call."

When I pick up my phone to call Brandon, I see a text from him.

Dear Rina,

Call me when you get a chance. We need to talk. I wish you hadn't flown to California.

Talk soon.

Brandon

"Hello."

"Hi, Brandon, I called as soon as I got your message."

"Hmm. Yeah, I was disappointed when I saw your text that you flew to California. I wish we could talk in person, but I guess this is what you want. Listen, Rina, I will always love you, but I don't think I can forgive you ever for not confiding in me."

"Brandon, you are not giving us a chance. I know how much I hurt you, but I think we can get to a point where forgiveness can happen. I love you and want to be with you."

"Rina, that's what you think. But your actions speak louder than words. I believe that my cousin means more to you than you even know. And the fact that he is the one person that I have despised my entire teenage years, makes it even more unforgivable. Life has a way of making decisions for us that we are not aware needs to be made. You made the decision to be with Marcus long before you came back to New York. I recognize the truth when it smacks me in the face, and you chose Marcus back then. Just admit it."

"Brandon, you are not being fair. I will admit that I have been confused about my feelings for Marcus, but it has nothing to do with us."

"You are wrong, Rina, it has everything to do with us! Let's just let it be. Don't worry about me. I will move my things out of the apartment before you get back. Take care, and I wish you the best." And he hangs up the phone.

I can't help but sit here in a stupor. Brandon's words weigh heavy on my mind, even though he had made the decision long before I called him. Life is full of surprises, and we have to be accountable for our own actions. I have to accept that our life as 'Brina' is over. And now I know what I need to do.

"Merry Christmas, Marcus. I happen to be visiting my sister, can we meet up somewhere and talk?"

I am hopeful for the choice that was made for me. But I can't help but think to myself, even though my relationship with Marcus began on 'Love at First Sight; he was not intended to be my bachelor.

Six months later
June 2020
Rina

Holding hands with Marcus, walking around the empty Santa Monica Pier, I still can't believe what has happened. The entire world is in a pandemic caused by the COVID-19 virus that originated in Wuhan, China. Millions of people have died just in the United States alone and that does not even include worldwide statistics. We are required to wear a mask whenever we leave our homes, and it is recommended to not leave our home unless absolutely necessary. Only essential businesses are allowed to stay open.

In-door dining has become a luxury of the past. Take-out food and ordering groceries online have become a novel pastime. The elderly and immune-compromised persons are the main target for this horrific virus. Families are asked not to visit their parents or grandparents. Initially, the country was asked to quarantine in their homes for six weeks. But, as none of us expected, the virus continued its rampage.

And, in the midst of this nightmare, Marcus and I found each other. Marcus and I met the next day after I texted him. I met him at his apartment and even though he had made this fantastic meal for us, I never made it past his front door. All I did was look into his face, when he smiled, and his twin dimples deepened, I became putty. His hand touched the side of my arm and across my collarbone. His other hand cupped my jaw, and he kissed me deeply, slowly, like he was drinking me in.

He picked me up, carried me to his bedroom, and gently laid me on top of his bed. Very slowly, he began to undress me, with no objection from me. He laid on top of me still clothed. I reached out to unbuckle his jeans, and he pulled my hand away. "Just let me admire you before we get down to business. I have done nothing but dream about this moment, and I want to take it all in."

He began to kiss every inch of my body beginning at the top of my head down to my toes. I was squirming like a snake ready to attack. The moans escaping from my mouth were embarrassing loud, but uncontrollable. Finally, he allowed me to undress him, and I tried to kiss every inch of him, too. But he had his own agenda in mind.

When he entered me, I had this sensation of being fulfilled at last. We made love with a frenzied rhythm which had both of us breathless at the end of the encounter. We both reached our climax simultaneously. Afterward, we both lay satiated on top of his covers, with me cradled in his arms. We laid like that for a long time. Finally, he adjusted himself on top of me and said, "Are you hungry yet?" I laughed. I am still not sure if he was asking if I wanted to make love again or eat.

That was the day that I decided to move to California. It was the right decision for several reasons. It would allow me to live close to my sister, work on my relationship with Marcus, and escape the disaster I made of my life with Brandon. I was proud of the fact that I wasn't running away from my problems, but actually, I am facing them head-on.

I flew back to New York and immediately started to pack all my belongings. I texted Brandon and told him that he is welcome to keep the apartment since I was moving out. I have no idea what he decided to do. We have not been in personal contact since that last conversation when he told me he could never forgive me although he will always love me. I think about him all the time and wonder how this pandemic has affected his life.

When I made the decision to stay in southern California, I called my boss and told her about my decision, and she wished me the best. She also gave me a high recommendation to their sister magazine, Styles in LA. I met with the senior editor that next week, and she agreed to let me be her protégé. I feel that it is as if all my stars have aligned, and I am living the life I have always dreamed of.

Thankfully, Susannah invited me to stay as long as I wanted at her home until I decided I needed my own space.

But now that COVID-19 has reared its ugly truth, I find myself working from Susannah's home, I sometimes wish for my own place. Marcus has offered his apartment to me should I feel the need to escape, but Susannah's home is so large, I never feel as though I have no privacy. When COVID-19 hit in March, I agreed to not see Marcus until the six-week quarantine was over. I chose to do this to keep baby Frankie and my sister safe.

But, after that six-week prison term, we have a system. We see each other just about every weekend. During the week, we both work from our own homes. Neither of us is taking the chance to be around others, who may infect us, and I feel that we are safe when we do meet up on the weekends. And today is one of those weekends.

"Marcus, do you think we will ever go back to life as it was before? Or will we have to deal with COVID-19 forever? Is this the new norm?"

"Sorry, Rina, I wish I had the answers to those questions. Sometimes I feel as though we are in a sci-fi movie and none of this is real. But then I wake up, and reality hits. But we have to look at the positive side of things. We both have good jobs and good health, one day there may be a COVID-19 vaccine. Yes, life may be a little different, but at least we have each other."

I smile and reach over to kiss him on the lips and whisper, "I am so happy that you are my bachelor, and no one else's."

ABOUT THE AUTHOR

Tricia Heggeness currently lives in La Quinta, California, and has been an avid reader all her life. Born in Hutchinson, Kansas, Tricia was raised as a Navy brat and moved from state to state with her family. To further her education after high school, she received a graduate degree in business administration from Central Michigan University.

While writing has been a favorite pastime; especially while raising her two daughters, Lisa and Greta, she has enjoyed traveling throughout Europe, with Italy being one of her favorite destinations. You may run into Tricia on one of her cruising vacations or you can also find her on a pickleball court or playing an occasional round of golf.

This is Tricia's first published novel, and she hopes her readers enjoy it.